On
Pointe

LORIE ANN
GROVER

Margaret K. McElderry Books
New York   London   Toronto   Sydney

Also by Lorie Ann Grover

Loose Threads

Margaret K. McElderry Books
An imprint of Simon & Schuster
Children's Publishing Division
1230 Avenue of the Americas
New York, New York 10020

Book design by Ann Sullivan
The text for this book is set in Mrs. Eaves.

Manufactured in the United States of America
2 4 6 8 10 9 7 5 3 1

Library of Congress Cataloging-in-Publication Data
Grover, Lorie Ann.
On pointe / Lorie Ann Grover.—1st ed.
p. cm.
Summary: In this novel written in free verse, Clare and her grandfather must deal with changes in their lives when Clare's summer growth spurt threatens to end her dream of becoming a ballet dancer and her grandfather suffers a stroke.
ISBN:1-4169-7826-7   ISBN-13: 978-1-4169-7826-8
[1. Ballet dancing—Fiction. 2. Grandfathers—Fiction.
3. Change—Fiction. 4. Self-perception—Fiction.] I. Title.
PZ7.G9305On 2004
[Fic]—dc21
2003009963

Dedicated to my grandfather,
Reuel Grant Garber,
who always said I felt the music;

and my husband,
David Warren Grover,
who saw the trees dancing.

Special thanks to
my mother, Karine Leary,
for driving me to ballet for ten years
and waiting through all those classes;

my brothers, Dale and Kevin Leary,
who had to come along
and wait as well;

and my editor, Emma Dryden,
who dances with me now
from one end of the manuscript
to the other.

Willow

I dance because Mother says I'm her prima ballerina. City Ballet Company? Please. I'm going to New York. Soon I'll be the youngest professional dancer in American Ballet Theatre. Mother says so.

Rosella

I dance because money won't buy my spot in City Ballet. I want this so bad I'll do anything. I get whatever I want.

Dia

I dance to feel beautiful. But all of a sudden I've grown. Not taller or fatter. But now I need a big bra and my hips are huge. I have to cover up and hide everything. Otherwise they won't let me dance anymore. I know it.

Margot

I dance because I always have. What else would I ever do?

Elton

Most guys don't dance, but I like to. None of my friends get it. Who cares? Ballet makes me strong. Besides, I like hanging out with so many girls.

Clare

I work half an hour at the barre and an hour on the floor, six days a week. I stretch every sinew and sweat from every pore, proving I'm in control. This is our dream: me, my mom, dad, and grandpa's. We dream that I'll be a dancer in City Ballet.

I let go of the barre,
press my salty lips
to my towel,
and breathe in my sweat.
Willow pitty pats her face dry.
Elton wipes up
where he dripped.

"Here, Clare."
Rosella hands me my toe shoes.
"Thanks."

"And now move to the floor room,"
says Madame.

Little girls
pour out of the dressing room,
racing for the barres
we've stepped away from.

We hurry with our class
down the hall
to the floor room
and watch the adult class end.
"How sad," whispers Rosella.
The men and women are like
twenty years old.
A few could be thirty or forty.
Who knows?

They don't use pointe shoes.
Their bodies sag.
Bits of fat
bounce on their bones.
Their tights and leotards
blare color.
Half of them can barely stumble
through combinations.
Their instructor with the little goatee
must be sick to his stomach
after trying to teach them.
Why are they even here?
Why do they smile?

I shrink back
as they brush by
to leave.

The guys get extra time to stretch
while we girls
drop down against the back wall.
Without our flat shoes on,
we are
a row of feet,
bulging in tights
spotted red and brown with blood.

The holes we cut

let us peel the fabric
back from our toes.
The tights tug up
loose skin and coagulated blood.
"Huhhhhh!"
We grind our teeth and blink back
the stinging pain.

Blisters pop.
Clear liquid runs.
Fresh blood oozes.

Gauze,
tape,
moleskin,
and spongy pink toe caps
hold the skin
and blood in place.

"Hppp!"
We hold our breath
and stretch
the tights
back over our toes.

Our feet slip
into satin shoes
with stiff shanks,
hard boxing,

tight elastic,
and slippery ribbons
that wrap and end
in hard knots.
The frayed edges
are crammed
out of sight.
We stand.

A row of bound feet
rises
to its toes.

"I'm looking
for a four/four piece,"
Madame says to the pianist,
the old guy
that's here everyday,
that no one ever talks to
or really looks at.
"No, not that one," says Madame.
She shuffles through his music.

Rosella and I
lean against the window.
A breeze tickles a couple stray hairs
against my cheek.
I press them back into place

and look outside.
The Cascade foothills
snug up close against my grandpa's town
sitting low in the valley.
Mount Rainier is peeking out
of the top of the clouds
hovering above us.
It looks huge.
"I'm definitely fat today, Clare," says Rosella.
"You are not," I whisper,
and look away from the window.
She turns sideways
and stares at herself in the mirrors
that cover the wall.
They show the truth
every second we are in this room.
But even so,
some girls can't see themselves
for real.
"Yes, I am," she says. "Fat."
I shake my head.
Even her neck
looks skinnier today.

"Okay, class."
Madame claps,
and we walk out to the floor.
None of us is fat.
Or

we wouldn't be here.

There are only
sixteen positions
in City Ballet.
Sixteen positions
make the company.
How many in my class?
How many in the conservatory?
How many in western Washington
dream
like me
to be
one
in sixteen?

We stand
perfectly still.
Madame chants the combination.
"Demi-plié, pas de chat, changement, relevé."
I try to mark the steps
by barely moving my hands.
We catch the words
being fired out
of her red-lined lips.
My mind is frantic

to gather each sound.
"Begin," she says.

The pianist plays an intro.
I dip down and leap, switch feet and rise
on pointe.
Repeat. Repeat. Repeat.
And then flow into the steps
we memorized last class.
The choreography is graceful, then strong.
It's like I'm melting,
then getting zapped with electricity,
then flowing across the floor.
To the final plié.
I got it.
Every single step.

I hold my arabesque.
Madame weaves through the class
making adjustments to form.

I'm at least four whole inches
taller than all the girls,
and a couple inches taller than all the boys,
except Elton.
He's still taller than me, at least.

Why didn't I inherit Mom's shortness

instead of Dad's tallness?
And why the spastic growth spurt
this summer?
My ankle wobbles,
and sweat outlines my eye.

Madame raises my foot.
Her eyes measure every edge of me.

Please, don't notice the four inches.

She moves on.
Her cane taps along the floor.
"Good, Margot."
I peek at her in the mirror.
Margot's only five-foot-two.
I lose my balance
and drop the arabesque.

We're
sliced and divided
into little groups.

If we're performing,
it's as a group
of individuals,
each dying to be noticed for something good.
I land my triple pirouette.

Madame doesn't see it.

If we're waiting our turn,
we're watching
to see if anyone
fails in any little way.
Willow misses a tendue.
Madame doesn't see it.

We're sliced and divided.

Dust.
Steamy sweat,
like a pot
of chicken soup.
Oak floors.
Pine rosin.
Sour breath
from deep inside.
We breathe it all
in rhythm.

Here is the moment
when the music flows into my bones,
and I don't have to
think of the steps,
and I don't have to count the movements,

and it really feels
like I might actually be
dancing
for a few seconds.

I'm a pale dust mote
swirling on a warm
sunbeam.
I leap and float,
land deep and rise
to step and spin in the shaft of light,
showing everyone
who I really am.
It's like
I'm turned
inside out.

With a great sweeping bow,
we thank Madame,
silently,
but for the brush of shoes on wood,
and then we bow
to ourselves in the mirrors.
Even if we failed most everything today,
at least these bows
let us pretend
we're real dancers.

Madame once was.
A dancer.
We all know she was great.
Her black-and-white photos line the back wall.
She was a soloist,
then a principal dancer
in a European company.
She lived it,
every person's dream in this room.
So even though
she's the typical ballet instructor—
tough,
harsh,
and scary—
we respect her
for what she was
and
what she can do for us
now.

I snatch my flat shoes
from the row against the wall.
It's easy to find
the biggest pair.
"Can you come over today, Rosella?"
She works at landing
a triple pirouette
and nails it.

"Rosella?"
"Oh, sorry.
No, not today.
My mom says this Saturday is hers.
She wants to go shopping with me."
"Okay."

Leaving the floor room,
I look back.
Dia is comparing herself
to Rosella
in the mirror.
Dia grew big breasts and hips
this spring.
She's tried to
shrink back to normal,
wearing sweaters
and rubber pants.
But nothing has worked.
Her body's out of control.
Everyone can see it.
Madame will speak
to her soon.
"It's pointless to think
you can achieve," she'll say.
Rumor is,
that's her standard line
before you get kicked out.
I clutch my shoes

and rush down the hall.
I can't keep growing
taller.
I've got to stop.
I can't lose control
and be pointless
like poor Dia.

Everyone bustles
around the dressing room.
Chiffon skirts,
shoes,
and ribbons
flutter
as we metamorphosize
back into girls
and cover up
our leotards and tights
with jeans and T-shirts.

"Rosella!"
I bang on the stall.
The toilet flushes.
She comes out
wiping her lips
on toilet paper.
"You don't

have to puke—" I say.
"Yes. I do."
I cross my arms and block her way.
"You don't, Rosella."
"Knock it off." She shoves by,
and I follow.
"You saw how fat I was in there, Clare.
It broke my whole entire line."
"Give me a break."
"No, give *me* one.
You're supposed to be my friend."
I raise my voice, "I am."
The other girls stare at us.
I glare at Rosella,
but she doesn't notice.
She crams her stuff in her bag
and leaves without looking back.

Rosella's mom waves to me
as Rosella climbs into their convertible.
They pull out into traffic,
so neither one sees me
wave back.

The crosswalk light
takes forever to change.
I stare at the red hand.
Finally it turns

to the walking person.
I jog across Main Street,
hurrying by the yellow daffodil silhouette
spray painted on the asphalt.
The flowers mark every intersection in town.
The crosswalk light changes
before I get to the curb,
like always.
I reach the sidewalk
as the cars roll over the painted flower.
Nearly all the nearby farms grow daffs.
Grandpa says once everyone grew hops
till disease took the crops.
I can't imagine beer mugs
painted at all the corners.

I brush gently against the heart-shaped leaves
trailing from the streetlight hanging baskets.
I smile at the judge watering his begonias
outside the Hammermaster Law Office.
He's the only judge in town,
so everyone recognizes him.
Even me,
just from visiting Grandpa so much.
"Hello," he says as water
splatters down onto the cement.
"Hi."
I walk past.

The splashing water sound reminds me of Rosella.
Yuck.
I could never puke like she does.
Even if I was overweight,
I'd eat less or something.
She eats less and vomits.
Where does she get energy
to get through class?
What am I supposed to do?
She's definitely getting worse.
Other girls do it every now and then,
but Rosella is puking
after every class.
What about at home?
Should I tell her mom
or mine?
My grandpa, since I'm living with him
this summer?
Madame?
I'm Rosella's friend.
She should listen to me.
I slip by the skinny tendrils dangling
from the last flower basket.
Or maybe I should listen to Rosella
and shut up?
She does have to stay thin. . . .

Grandpa's house and garden

are surrounded by
a tall laurel hedge.
Sometimes, before I walk through
the little iron gate,
the shrubs look mean,
like they are trying to keep me out.
But other times,
the shrubs are like big arms
waiting to hug me into Grandpa's house.

Today I step through the gate
easily.
The garden flowers sway
in the late afternoon wind.
Even the house's sloping Tudor roof
looks like a lopsided smile.
I race up the porch steps
and open the storm door.
Classical music
plays softly
for Mija,
his sixteen-year-old black cat.
Today the hedge and house
seem just right.

"I'm home, Grandpa!"
"Hello, love," he calls from the back porch.
I pour a big glass of orange juice
and nuke a bag of fat-free popcorn.

I stretch out on the couch.
Mija manages to leap up,
nibbles a piece I dropped,
then stretches and arches her back.
She slinks down
and disappears around the corner
with perfect grace,
despite her crickety old self.

Grandpa comes in and sits
in his small velvet chair.
"How was dancing today, Clare?"
"Class
was fine," I answer.
"Did you express yourself
with those fast spins on one leg?"
"Fouettés. Yeah."
"Excellent. There's nothing like dance.
When your grandmother was alive,
she and I ruled
the ballroom."
I zone out.
I've heard this a thousand times.
I barely remember my grandma.
She died when I was little.
Finally he finishes.
He smiles and crosses his legs.
"Pass the popcorn, please."

I do.
Only a couple kernels
roll around on the bottom of the bowl.
"You are a scoundrel," he says.
"My couch, my juice, and all my popcorn."
"But I'm your granddaughter." I grin.
"That you are, Clare."
He runs his bumpy finger
around the bowl.
"You don't need that salt, Grandpa."
He raises an eyebrow above his glasses
and licks his finger clean.
"You're right," he says. "One more lick."

I dump our empty microwave dinner plates
into the garbage.
Enough time left for a bath.
"Night, Grandpa." I kiss him
on the forehead.
"Night, Clare." He slips back to sleep
in his chair.

In the pink-and-black bathroom,
I peel off my cold leotard and tights
like a layer of skin.
While the soaking powder dissolves in the water,
I sit on the chilly toilet lid

and pick the tape off my toes.
I step into the tub.
Yikes! It burns, burns, burns
the open sores
on my feet.
Then it stops.
Hey.
The tub seems shorter
than ours at home.
I shiver
in the hot water.

Everyone is sacrificing
so my dream to dance
with City Ballet
comes true.
Mom and Dad pay for shoes, clothes, and lessons.
Grandpa helps pay for them too,
and lets me live here for the summer.
So much money is spent on me,
I have to sacrifice
my whole body.
I can't waste a dime.

I dial,
tug the sheet
up between my legs,

and leave my throbbing feet poking out.
The cool night air slips around the room,
but I'm too beat to get up and close the windows.
I don't know if I have enough energy
to even talk to Mom.
But here goes.

"Hello?"
"Hi, Mom."
"Clare! How was class?
Was it fun and energizing?
Did you do well?"
"It was fine."
"Great! And
is everything going smoothly
with your grandfather?
Are you two still getting along?
No problems now, I hope."
"No, we're doing okay.
It's still easier staying here
than taking the bus every day
from our apartment."
"That was the plan.
A good plan.
I knew it would be.
You're getting the best instruction
right in my old hometown.
I'll never figure out
how Ballet Conservatory

ended up there.
Someone liked the setting,
I suppose,
at some point.
So there you have it.
And it's all worked out for us.
Tell me,
how are your new shoes holding up?"
"They're okay.
Mostly.
I, um, I'll need another pair
in a couple weeks."
"I'll put in the order, Clare.
Happy to do it for you."
"Sorry I'm wearing them out so quickly."
"Now, now. None of that.
Anything for our dream.
Any word on the audition, sweetheart?
You must be so excited.
I bet it's only days away.
I understand
they wait to post the announcement
till just before the tryouts,
to keep nerves at bay.
So, Clare,
have you heard yet?"
"Not yet, Mom." I scrinch the sheet
into my fist.
She talks a hundred miles a second

through every minute.

"Well, when all goes as planned,
are you ready to spend the school year
with Grandpa?
It would be a perfect ~~~~~~ ~u.
Think abou~ —"
"Definite~
It's close
Rosel~
And
a to
"No
ballet
for frie~
But then, ~~~~~~~~~~~~ ~dable,
and you do h~
She's such a dear."
"Yeah. But, Mom?"
"Yes?"
"I would miss working at the bookstore
with you and Dad."
"That's nice of you to say, Clare.
But like we discussed,
you could come home after class
occasionally,
on Saturdays,
and earn some money."
"That'd be good."
"I drove by your and Rosella's

old dance school today.
You both have certainly outgrown
their little yearly performances for parents."
"Definitely."
"And now you are at the conservatory,
ready to audition
for City Ballet Company.
Next it will be Pacific Northwest Ballet,
or even New York City, Clare!
Our dream is about to come true, honey!"
"Mom, you sound like a sappy commercial."
"Well, I'm so proud!
But since it's late, I'll let you go.
You need to get your rest."
I let go of the sheet
and try to smooth it out.
"Oh, and Dad sends his love, Clare."
"Love to him too."
"And he says to remind you, 'Work hard.
Failure is not in your future.'"
"Yeah. Right." Dad's favorite line. "Night, Mom."
"Good night, my little ballerina."
Click.
Little?
Ballerina?

Why can't Mom focus
on one thing?

Why can't I think about City Ballet
without the pressure of PNB
or some New York company
in the way far-off future?
City Ballet is what I'm working for.
Isn't that enough, Mom?

"Clare," Grandpa calls
through my bedroom door
in the morning.
"Clare."
I don't answer
and wait for him to give up.
He cracks the door
and peeks in.
I close my eyes and lie
perfectly still.
He closes the door
and heads out to church.
Every week he tries this.
I take class six days out of seven.
Let me at least chill out on Sunday!
Even Mom said I didn't have to go to church.
Everyone agreed to that
before I moved in.
We've never gone.
Why should I start
because I'm staying with Grandpa?

I snuggle down
under my covers.

After I wake and eat lunch,
I go out and weed
in Grandpa's garden.
I rip out the clover enthusiastically
to make up for not going with him.

"Hi." I wave as Grandpa pulls in.
"What're you doing there, Clare?"
"Some weeding." I beam,
ready for sure praise.
"Oh." He shuts the car door.
"Want to help me?"
"No. But thanks. I don't work
on the Lord's Day."
The trowel slips from my muddy hand.
"Oh, right. Sorry."
"Why don't you come in,
and we'll have a simple lunch."
"I—I already ate."
He nods and goes inside.

Ugh. I stab the dandelion roots
with the weeder stick
and yank the plant out of the dirt.
I heave it at the wheelbarrow.
Why can't I ever seem to do the right thing

to please Grandpa?

He naps
then goes back to church at night.
For evening service
he doesn't bother knocking on my door.
Just leaves me a note saying
he'll eat dinner with his friends
afterward,
and I can find something
in the freezer.
I hide out in my room
through the afternoon.
Reading and napping to avoid him
till he leaves again.
Come on.
Everyone needs a down day.
Right?

"Morning."
"Morning, love."
Since Sunday's over,
everything will be normal again between us.
Not weirdo stressed.
It's been the pattern since I moved in.
Grandpa's smiling,
which helps me smile back.

I kiss his cheek
and smell warm prune juice.
Yuck.
He dabs his mouth. "Aha!"
"What?"
He fills in the last squares
on his crossword.
"Not in unison is *discordant.*"

I stir my breakfast drink.
This is it for me.
Rosella vomiting makes me feel too guilty
to eat anything else.
"D-i-s-c-o-r-d-a-n-t," he spells.
"When something doesn't fit in
with the rest. Like a note in music."
He looks up at me.
"Right," I say.
Discordant.
Like one girl who's taller
than the rest.
The skin on my back
crawls against my T-shirt.

My tights squeeze my legs.
My leotard encases my body.
I wind my ponytail tighter and tighter
and pin it to my head.

I'm a ballet student
who feels like a lean linked
sausage.

I shove over the covers,
sit on my bed,
and cut foot holes
in my new tights.
Snip, snip.

Perfect.
Just the right size.
And the tights aren't running.
At least something on me
is perfect today.
Even if
nobody will see.

Yeah.
It'll be fun to spend the school year
at Grandpa's.
I like the little town,
and I've always loved this house.
The same one Mom grew up in.
It has a rich full smell
with smooth wood floors.
The small window panes
make things look ripply

because the glass is curvy,
from 1926,
when the house was built.
I love all Grandpa's family's antiques
that were passed down to him,
like the iron bed
and antique dresser in here.
And now this room,
which used to be the guest one,
looks like mine:
clothes on the floor,
bed unmade,
stuffed animals
lining the wide baseboard,
books overflowing the shelves,
and the giant poster of Mikhail Baryshnikov,
the perfect dancer of all time—
and drop-dead gorgeous, Rosella and I say.
This room feels like mine
already.

By the time I double stitch
a torn ribbon on my toe shoe
and snip the loose threads,
Grandpa's calling me to eat lunch.
The protein bar
should hold me through class.
"You sure that's enough food, Clare?"

"Yes," I say with my mouth full.
If he only knew what Rosella gets by on.

Grandpa pats my back
as I head out the door.
"Bye, Clare.
Have a good time."
I turn and wave until he goes inside.
The air is still cool.
My clogs crunch the fir needles,
sending a Christmas smell
out into the summer air.
I weave through the garden.
I piqué and glissade
where no one can see me.
I jeté around the giant sunflowers.
A chickadee
hops in the birdbath.
One last double pirouette,
and I'm out the gate,
onto the sidewalk.
Nothing is better
than Grandpa's garden.

I dig out the dill pickle
I stashed in my bag earlier,
unwrap it,

and take a big bite.
Mmmm.
Not many calories and delicious!
I munch and cut through the alley
behind the bakery and gift shops
to avoid the window shoppers.
I try not to kick up dirt
onto my tights.
I run across Main
when the traffic breaks.
The last bite of pickle
makes me burp garlic.

Up the front staircase,
I pull hard
on one of the heavy wooden doors
and step into the brick conservatory
that pulses with music
and movement.
The door thuds closed.
My heart skips a beat
and is out of sync
with everything around me.

In the foyer
I smooth my hair
and mash my bun

until I feel the bobby pins
jab into my scalp.
Hairspray sticks to my fingers.
I press one stray pin
back into the center.
It pops halfway out again.
I press it in,
but it won't stay.
I shoulder my bag,
pull the bobby pin all the way out,
pry it open with my teeth,
and shove it into the other side
of my bun.
Sometimes
things don't stay
how you want them.

With a deep breath,
I step into the barre room,
where the adult class teeters
to keep their balance.
The instructor looks over at me.
"And hold it, hold it,"
he directs them.
I cast my eyes down
and rush along the opposite wall
to get to the dressing room.

This place has a lousy design.
People are always coming through
at the end of someone else's session
to change and get ready for their class.
Everyone knows to scurry by silently.
Even if it is
just the adults.

In the dressing room,
I glance sidelong at Ellen;
she's looking at Margot,
who's sneaking a peek at that new girl, Devin.
Rosella's not here yet.
Except for me and her,
no one's really friends
with anyone else.
Ballet students at the conservatory
don't hang out at each other's houses
or even call to chat.
The only time we speak
is to ask
to borrow a bandage
or to say, "Excuse me,"
before pushing past.
Everyone is someone
trying to be better
than you.

It's risky to make friends.
Or to care.

Rosella and I met
back in kindergarten.
My mom drove me across town
to an uppity preschool.
The only really good thing about it
was Rosella.
We've been friends
since the first day.
We both drew ballerinas
in the art corner.
We took classes together for years
at our old ballet school.
Sharing the same dream when you're kids
is fun.
But here,
everyone is completely serious.
Each person at the conservatory
shares our dream.
Each is a threat,
trying to be one in sixteen.
If sixteen of them
make it,
my dream dies.

I slip off my jeans and T-shirt
and tie on my black chiffon miniskirt.

I kick off my clunky clogs
for thin, leather, flat shoes
that glove my feet.

My bones and muscles
poke out all over.

Here
everything has to be uncovered.

Margot walks by
in the dressing room,
wearing nothing
but a dangling tampon string.

Is she so used
to people staring
at her body,
correcting and directing,
that she believes
it doesn't matter
if anyone looks anymore?

Is she so confident
of her body
that anyone can look

at everything?

Why am I the only one
blushing?

Willow never gets ready alone.
Her mother swoops into the dressing room
for final touches,
like a splash of rose water.
We are bumped aside
for Willow's completion.
"There." Her mother sighs.
"Now go dance,
my prima ballerina."
Willow parades out to the barre room,
wearing the only smile around.

Yeah, my mom might call me
her little ballerina,
but at least she doesn't smother me
like Willow's mom.
Shoving in,
telling me what to do
and how to get better.
That's got to be a ton of pressure for Willow.
Her mom needs a life.
At least mine's got the bookstore with Dad.

She has something other than me.
Doesn't she?

Willow's mom scuttles out
while Rosella charges in.
"I guess Prima
is ready for class," she mutters.
"Mommy made her smell like a rose today."
Rosella snorts.
If we throw our anger at Willow,
we can pretend we didn't argue yesterday.
"I didn't eat yet." Rosella dumps her stuff
and peels open a yogurt container.
I fight my smile
because she's making an effort to eat.
I retie my skirt.
She gulps the pink stuff down until
we hear Margot retching in the bathroom.
"See, I'm not the only one." Rosella smirks.
"Whatever." I hope she'll eat more.
The toilet flushes,
and Margot walks by us
straightening her leotard.
Her pale face
stretches over her
sharp cheekbones.
Rosella tosses her half-eaten yogurt
into the garbage.

Thunk.
We both
follow Margot
out of the dressing room.

The barre
is cool
under my hot fingertips.
I choose a place
to stand.
Point hard, and harder.
I crunch the top of my toes
under.
One foot
and then the other.
First position,
turned out from the hip
as far as I can go
without my feet rolling inward.
My turn-out is
better than Rosella's,
but not as good as Margot's.
We haven't even begun,
and I know how I measure up.
I have to work harder.
I slide my hand forward
to a cooler spot.

We each feel it.
Without mirrors in the barre room,
we can't check ourselves.
Even the girls who don't believe what they see
want to look in a mirror.
I twist and check out my rear.
My leotard's creeping.
I snap the elastic.
Dia stretches
to be sure her short chest sweater
stays down.
Willow examines her plié
and adjusts her turn-out.
Rosella reties her skirt.
She's measuring to see if her waist
is bigger.
All of us wonder if
we look okay
without mirrors
saying so.
We for sure can't ask
each other.

Black leotard—
V neck,
square back,
high-cut legs;
pink tights—

not too pink,
not too white,
no underwear
but a thin bra;
chiffon skirt—
cut from one piece
of cloth;
optional leg warmers
with a foot strap;
rubber pants or short sweaters
if you've gained a pound;
flat ballet slippers
for barre work;
European custom toe shoes
for floor exercise;
a bun;
no bangs;
no jewelry;
no identity.

No one
breaks the silence
until
Tommy and Elton come out
of the boys' dressing room.
"You are kidding!" says Tommy.
"Nope." Elton grins.
They bust up laughing

and join the other boys at the barre.
"What?" asks Nathan.
Tommy fills him and the other guys in.
I wonder what it's like
in their dressing room.
They obviously talk and have fun.
There's so much less competition
for guys.
A company needs every good male
it can find.
I bet
no one vomits,
and their feet never bleed
since they don't work on pointe.
It's so much easier
for them.
Even if people wonder if they are gay.

That's probably why Tommy
hits on every new girl—
to prove he's straight.
He acted so into Devin last week,
he nearly got kicked out of class
for whispering.
Devin never did look interested.
All the girls have dealt with Tommy.
Except me.
I'm so much taller,
he never looks my way.

No one has gone out with him.
We all would have heard if someone had.
Even girls who don't talk to each other
would have whispered about that.
It would have been too juicy to resist.

Going out
makes studying dance too complicated.
There's no way to focus
when you're so into each other.
Willow's mother was all over her
when she caught Willow flirting with Nathan.
The way she was bending over so close to him,
pretending to retie her ribbons.
Willow shrunk in the dressing room
while her mother ranted.
She doesn't even stand near Nathan now.

I look over at Elton.
He never chases anyone, girls or guys.
Only seems sure of himself,
like now,
stretching at the barre.
He turns my way and smiles.
I super quick
look away.

Madame sweeps

into the room.
Her thin legs glide
in a permanent turn-out.
Her thinner cane
raps the floor
in four/four time,
even without music.
One penciled eyebrow rises.
"Pliés," she commands.
The barre room pianist
is a big younger woman.
So different from the floor room
old guy.
But the music sounds the same,
and no one notices her much either.
She pings out the tune
as we grow taller
in preparation
for pliés
for Madame.

Sinking down
in an open knee bend,
then standing up.

Plié, first,
second,

fourth,
fifth.
Relevé.
Turn.
Plié, first,
second,
fourth,
fifth.

It takes total control
to sink down all the way
and come up again.

My développé begins to shake;
the tiniest tremor
crawls up my outstretched leg
raised to hip level.

Madame strikes her cane on the barre.
Snap!
I jerk.
She barely missed my fingers.
"Higher, Clare," she demands.
My mouth is pasty.
A tendon cramps
along my groin
as I lift my leg

one-fourth of an inch
higher.
But Madame has passed.
Hasn't even waited to see.
The sweat sears
my eye.

"Good extension, Willow,"
Madame croons.
My leg shakes violently
while I stare
at Willow's short, still leg
poised at shoulder height.

"And end,"
says Madame.
I try to control my long leg
as it comes crashing down.
Only a moment
to rub the cramp.
"Other side,"
Madame demands.

Endless
left,
right,
up,

down,
turn,
again,
to warm up
and get ready
to learn to dance
in the floor room.

"Want to get a soda
after class, Clare?"
"Sure."
I follow Rosella
and drag my hand
on the long hallway windowsill.
I guess she's totally over my confronting her
about puking.
Since we both heard Margot,
I'll act like it's no big deal too.
"Yeah, that sounds good."
"Great." She stops outside the floor room.
"My mom's going to be half an hour late
because of a salon appointment."
"Okay."
We stand aside for the adult class
to leave.
The last woman, with fuzzy red hair,
finally gets her stuff together.

She says hello to our class
gathered by the door.
I look down and away,
not wanting to be linked to a loser.
No one answers but Elton.
"Hey, Janet," he says back.
How does he know her name?
I peek as she walks away,
dragging her hand on the sill
all the way down
the hall.

In this room
we can
search
for fat.
Our eyes
move over
our outlines
as we turn,
pose,
stretch a leg,
lift an arm.
Then, slyly,
we look for fat
on each other.

I crunch
a chunk
of golden rosin.
The pine scent
circles me
with confidence.
Crunch, crunch.
The ball of my foot
pulverizes
the yellow crystal
into white powder.
I rock the magic
onto my toe,
then do my heel.
I step out
and put the other toe in.
This stickiness will hold me
to the floor.
It will grip the wood
when I come flying down.
I can't believe my feet
have outgrown the rosin box.
I hurry away
before anyone sees.

Sliding down
into a split.
Rocking a bit

to let my thigh
open.
Leaning forward.
Forehead to knee.
Chest pressing
into my thigh.

Pushing up.
Lifting and shifting
to split in the middle.
Walking my hands
forward.
My breath condenses
into a mist
on the cool floor.
My chest touches
with each inhale.

Walking my hands
up again.
Lifting and shifting.
Splitting the other leg.
Wiping the sweat off
with my damp towel
while sitting,
sitting,
sitting
in my split.

Run, run, run, grand jeté.
Run, run, run, grand jeté.
My turn.
Run, run, run, grand jeté,
and time stops.
I'm at the highest point,
doing a split in the air
above everyone.
I hold it,
defying time and gravity.
"Look at me!" I want to yell.
My heart thumps,
and I glide to the floor.
I step to the back of the line.
Elton turns and whispers,
"Beautiful!"
I can't stop myself
from smiling up at him.
Which feels doubly great.
He *is* way taller than me.

I turn off Rosella's cell phone.
Grandpa said no problem
to me hanging out at the coffee shop.
"Good class." Rosella sips her diet soda.
I dunk my tea bag.
"It was. My calves are still burning."
"That last combination was a killer," she says.

"Yeah."
"Did you see Nathan fall out of his pirouette?"
"Totally."
"I thought Madame
was going to beat him with her cane."
"While he was down," I add.
"Elton sure looked good."
"Really?" I tuck my ballet bag
under my chair.
"He was totally checking you out
while we were stretching." She smiles.
"Nuh uh." I nudge her foot,
and she nudges me back.
The latte machine hisses.
We both look out the window.
Dia's mom's car pulls over
and picks her up
outside the conservatory.
"Man, I can't imagine being Dia," says Rosella.
"I know." I squeeze my tea bag
until it stops dripping
and wipe my fingers
on a napkin. "There's no way
she'll be able
to take pas de deux classes in the fall."
Rosella laughs. "Right!
No guy would ever be able to lift her."
I nod.
Will Elton be able to lift me?

He is really buff.
"Dia's studied for like ten years." Rosella
bites her straw.
"Same as us," I add.
"How could anyone have known
her body'd change like that. Her mom's a stick."
"She is small."
"Dia must weigh
a hundred twenty-five pounds," says Rosella.
The tea burns my mouth. "Ouch!"
I dab my lips. "Well, I weigh
one thirty, you know."
Rosella looks up quick.
"Oh, yeah. But that's because—"
"I'm so tall." I cross my legs
and try to tuck them
under the little bistro table.
My knee bangs the edge
and rocks everything.

"Lots of companies have taller girls," says Rosella.
"Mmm hmm."
"Like Pacific Northwest Ballet."
"Right. PNB. I've heard that."
"Don't worry, Clare."
"No, I'm not."
Oh, sure.

"My my, Clare." Rosella's mom
looks over the top of her designer sunglasses.
"You really have shot up."
I step back.
"Your father is tall, isn't he?"
"Yeah."
"Tt, tt." She shakes her head.
"See you tomorrow." Rosella gets in the car
and shuts her mom up.
"Bye."
They pull away.
I bypass the sidewalk
and turn down the deserted alley
to get out of sight.
I kick a stone.
It smacks a trash can.
Ping!
What does it matter
how a person looks
if she wants to
be a dancer?
I'm nearly as good
as everyone else in class.
I wipe my nose on my shoulder.
Down the road Grandpa's huge fir trees
jab into the sky.
I jab the air with my fist.
I do chaîné turns
and kick grands battements.

Pow, pow, pow!
My bag swings wild.
My right clog flies off.
Clunk.
It rolls across the pavement
into the weeds.
I hop over to get it
and cram it on.
Ouch!
I hobble down the alley.
It shouldn't matter what you look like
if you really want to dance.
I
want
to.

"Why the frown?"
Grandpa turns off the hose.
"No reason." I flop onto the porch swing
and kick my bag toward the front door.
He tamps the dirt around the daisies
with his foot
and gathers the hose.
The green coil tries to twist its own way,
but he carefully bends it
to make a pile of circles.
"There." He stretches his back
and wipes his hands on a rag.

"Tell me what's the matter, love."
He comes over behind me and rocks the swing.
"What if, for some reason,
I don't get to be a dancer?"
He doesn't say anything.
"I know Mom says
everything is going to work out,
and Dad says work hard
and failure's not in my future. But
stuff changes sometimes."
Creak.
Creak.
"It does. But in your case—" he starts.
"Grandpa, I've grown so—"
"Clare,
you already
are a dancer."
Creak.
Creak.
Creak.
I sigh out the sorrow
so the shaky tears don't come.
"Think about it," he says,
and walks away
without saying
anything else.

I pick the pins

Out of my bun
and tug out the elastic.
My brown hair
tumbles down
past my shoulders.
My scalp throbs.
I hunch a bit to look at myself
in the antique dresser mirror.
I've got
the little head,
the long neck,
the long arms,
and the little bust.
But my hips
are getting wider,
no question.
I squeeze them
between my hands.
"Stop growing!" I hiss.
And when I stand up straight,
I can't even see
my face anymore
in this mirror.
I have to tilt the mirror up far.
It's not just my hips.
The worst part is
my whole stupid body
is growing.
I'm totally out of control.

I flop on the bed.
I'm sickening.

Grandpa doesn't know anything.
Already a dancer?
Yeah. Right.

"For this food
we give thanks.
Let it nourish our bodies
and make us continue to grow
in stature, health, and grace.
Amen."
I stare across the table at him.
He stares back at me
until I look down.
Talking back to my grandfather
is not allowed.
Maybe a German-Swiss thing.
No matter
if he's completely wrong.
I ball my napkin on my lap
and rip little shreds off
where he can't see.

Grandpa and I
eat our mac and cheese

in silence.
Our spoons clack
against the frozen food plastic divider
keeping our peas separate.
Margot and Rosella would never eat the fat
on this plate.
Maybe a salad, no dressing or extras.
Lettuce and a carrot.
Or a skinless chicken breast, broiled.
Then they'd live it up
with fat-free Jell-O.
But right now
I don't even care.
This tastes good.
That's one thing about being taller.
Extra weight doesn't show as fast on me
as it does on the rest of them.
My spoon scrapes the black plastic plate
clean.

Ugh.
The ice cream did it.
In front of the mirror in my room,
my stomach
pooches out.
Like Mom's.
Fat. Fat. Fat.
What was I thinking?

Mac and cheese and ice cream?
Call me lard butt.

I kneel
and tuck my hair behind my ear.
My reflection wobbles in the toilet water.
I can do this.
Margot does it.
Rosella does it.
I knew not to tell anyone about her
because there's nothing wrong with it.
Right?
Plus, fewer calories
could mean I'd grow slower.
Couldn't it?
I can get rid of the ice cream, at least.
My fingernail scrapes the roof of my mouth
and pushes into the back of my throat.
Uckgh.
Rap, rap.
I drop the lid. *Bam.*
"Clare?"
"Yes." I swallow
and quick, dry my finger on my T-shirt.
"Are you all right?"
"Yes, Grandpa." I flush the clean water
and open the door.

"I'm fine."

I couldn't do it.
Even if Grandpa hadn't come to the door.
I sucked in twenty-four grams of fat.
Then I couldn't even puke it out.
What kind of dancer could I ever be?
Mija curls
at the foot of my bed.
Her breathing is rattly tonight,
but her weight and warmth
on my calves
seep through the sheet.
My feet ache
a little less.
I take a deep, relaxing breath
and let it out slowly.
Cats
equal comfort.

Running from the barre room
to the floor room
to the barre room
to the floor room
and back.
I can't find my class.

Only the fuzzy red-headed woman is there.
I keep passing her in the hallway.
And she is trying to tell me something,
but I won't listen to her.
I run and look for my class
all through my dream.

"I'm off to my theology book club, Clare."
"Okay, Grandpa."
"Eat a good brunch before you leave to dance."
"I will."
"See you later."
"Okay."
His shoes clud across the wood floor
to the front door.
He locks the deadbolt for me.
I roll over in bed
and bury my head
under my pillow.
I slept in,
and I'm exhausted.

The scale says 131.
I can work that pound off in class,
if I barely eat before I go in.
Sleeping through breakfast helped.
That just leaves lunch.

Orange juice
and dry toast
is all I deserve.
I'm off to a good start today.
Even if
I'm sluggish.
A cup of Grandpa's instant coffee
should zoom me up.
I grimace it down.

The City Ballet audition announcement
is tacked to the bulletin board.
It's on Saturday!
Four days away!
Mom was right about posting it close to the day.
They do like to pop it on us.
Everyone's excitement
bings around the dressing room.
The girls actually talk to each other.
Rosella's not here yet.
I pull on my slippers
and get caught up in the chatter.
"Are you going to—" asks Devin.
"For sure," I cut her off.
"Aren't you?"
"Of course.
That's why I'm taking classes here."
"I heard Willow's not," says Michaela.

"No way," three of us say at once.
"Yeah. Her mother's flown the prima
to New York
to audition for the ABT school."
"Get out! American Ballet Theatre?"
squeals Devin.
"For real. My cousin lives next door to her
and had to hear all about it."
"Well, that's less competition for us," I add.
"I'd be totally happy
to just make it into City Ballet," says Ellen.
"Me too," agrees Devin.
"But I have to get down
to a hundred pounds." Ellen
tugs on some rubber pants.
"I'm shooting for ninety-five." Devin
sucks in her stomach.
Dia comes in,
and everyone hushes.
We watch as she reads
the audition announcement.
There's no way she can make it
with her body.
She turns away and changes,
cowering in the corner
till she gets all her floppy bulges
covered up completely.
None of us can talk about the audition now.
And definitely

not to Dia.

Everyone pushes out the door
to the barre room.
Rosella bumps through them.
"Hi, Clare."
"Look." I point to the audition notice.
"Yes!" She punches her palm.
"Finally we'll be dancers
in City Ballet."
Her excitement makes me grin.
Maybe she's right.
We are both really good.
Maybe other tall girls around the city
will try out too.
I could be average for all I know!
Rosella stuffs everything under a chair
and grabs her shoes. "Come on!"

Dia can't find a place
at the barre.
No one wants to be next to her.
Like her freakishness
could rub off onto them
or something.
"Here,
Dia.

Here's a space," I say,
and make room.
She almost smiles.
"Thanks, Clare."
I start to smile back
until Rosella gives me a look.
"What?" I mouth.
She shakes her head
and looks away.

Some days
barre work
flies past
fast
with hardly any pain.
And then
other days
it's one long pain.
Today it's fast.
My mind
is thinking of Saturday's audition,
and my body exercises
itself.

The boys are as psyched
as the girls.
Everyone is pouring sweat.
Tommy is completely focused for once.

Elton tremors to keep his leg raised high.
I try to meet his extension
and almost do.
The guys are going to be fighting just as hard
as the girls for spots in City Ballet.
I give it my all to lift my leg a bit more . . .
and I do!
Look out. I'm fighting too.

"Dia, I'd like to
speak to you privately
before floor exercises begin,"
says Madame. "Continue to stretch, class."
We all stop moving.
Only our sweat
plops to the floor.

We watch
Madame and Dia
go into the office.

One of the ladies
from the adult class dashes back in.
It's the red-headed one
from my dream.
"Forgot my towel."
She giggles.
"Have a good dance," she calls to us and leaves.

"Like, who was she talking to?"
Rosella humphs.

The office door opens.
Madame glides to the front of the room.
She clicks out a combination.

During fouettés,
while I spin
round and round on pointe,
I see Dia rush out.
She is a blur.
But I see her go.
I'm sure
it's for good.

The rumors are already
buzzing.
"I heard her crying!" says Ellen.
"Madame told her she was too fat!"
Michaela adds.
"She said, 'Don't ever come back!'" Devin says.
I shove my stuff
into my bag.
I bang the stall door
and raise my voice over Rosella's stupid retching.
"Bye."
"Wait, Clare—"

But I don't.
I hurry away
from their fascination
of someone's dream dying.
It's like it fills them up,
or maybe it's their relief
bubbling out
that they haven't been cut too.

I run out of the conservatory,
away from my fear
of becoming Dia.

Today Grandpa's hedge
seems to reach out and smother me.
I hurry through the gate
and toss my bag in the house.
I grab a diet soda from the fridge
and sneak out to the backyard deck
without running into Grandpa.
How will Dia
stop ballet lessons?
Ten years of training
wasted.
What will she tell her parents?
The soda can sweats
in my hand.
What do you do

if they don't let you
learn to dance?

Grandpa comes around the house
with his wheelbarrow.
"How was dancing today?"
he asks without looking at me.
"Fine," I answer.
"Good." He dumps everything
into the recycle bin.
"They posted the audition
for City Ballet," I say,
and pull a splinter
out of the deck step.
Grandpa stretches his back.
"That's nice."
"It's on Saturday," I add.
"So you'll be auditioning?"
He turns and looks at me.
An image of Dia
rushing out
goes through my mind.
"Of course, Grandpa.
I want to become a dancer."
"Clare . . ."
A waxwing bird
swoops down into the bath,
ruffles his feathers,

and flies off.
"I wish you could believe me," he says quietly.
"You already *are* a dancer.
You have the same passion
your grandmother had
when she stepped out onto the floor.
You feel the music.
I've sat in on plenty of your classes
over the years
to see your dancing spirit.
You have to dance
when the piano—"
"Grandpa . . ." I get up and go inside.
My stomach rolls.
I dump my soda
down the sink
and smash the can flat.

"Auditions are on Saturday, Mom."
"Oh, sweetheart.
How exciting!
I know you'll do wonderfully.
Our dream is about to come true, isn't it?"
I bite a hangnail on my pinkie
and spit out the skin.
Mija winds around my ankles.
"I hope."
"Well, I'm certain it's all about to happen.

How's your grandpa?
Is he doing okay?
Is he feeling fine?"
"Yes." He walks by the kitchen window
with a rake. "He's been doing the usual.
He works in his garden
and goes to his Bible studies.
But sometimes . . ."
"What?
Clare,
tell me what you were going to say."
"Well, he talks on and on."
"Oh, Clare. Is that all?
Be patient with him.
He's lonely."
"I know. But it can drive me crazy."
"Clare—"
"Yeah, I know." I turn around
and lean against the counter.
Mija sits and washes her face.
"Has he been taking his medicine?
Regularly?"
"I think so.
Uh huh. Morning and night."
"Good. Now, are you really okay
with your dad and me
going to this booksellers' convention?
We won't be nearby
for the audition."

"Sure, Mom."
"Promise to call the cell phone
and let us know
the minute you finish."
"Okay."
"And be patient with Grandpa."
"I will."
"I need to go now, honey."
"Um."
"Is there something else, Clare?
Something on your mind?"
"Can I talk to Dad, Mom?"
"Well, he's busy with a customer right now.
But I could—"
"Oh, never mind. Love you, Mom. Bye."
"Love you too."
Click.
Bzzzz.
"It's just that
Dia got kicked out
and won't ever be a dancer,
and what if that happens to me?
Would you ask Dad that for me, Mom?"
Bzzzz.
"What if I'm too tall to make it?
Will everyone
still love me if I fail
at our dream?"
Bzzzz.

I hang up the phone.
Mija stares up at me.
"Even though I'm trying hard,
failure
could be
my future."

Grandpa
flicks through the channels.
I switch my split
from my right leg forward
to my left.
With the audition on Saturday,
a little extra stretching
won't hurt.
Even in pajamas.
"Be all that you can be,"
sings the commercial.
Grandpa waits for the soldier
to salute the flag
before he changes the channel.
Every now and then
he does something like that
that reminds me he was a soldier
in the Army once.
Before he worked for and retired
from Boeing Aerospace.
He carried the radio for his unit

in the Korean war.
Ages ago.
Not that he ever talks about it.
But his medals are displayed in the glass cabinet.
The jingle keeps going
in my brain.
Be all that you can be.
What's the best I can be?
Grandpa stops a second on PBS.
"Oh, Clare. This used to be your favorite show."
I split in the middle and grimace.
A big hairy monster
is telling a little yellow ball
she can grow up and do anything
she dreams of
if
she believes and tries hard enough.
"Grandpa," I complain.
"Okay, okay." He chuckles.
"So grown up now."
He starts channel surfing again.

I wonder if Dia
ever watched that show
when she was little?

"Do they hurt, Clare?"
"What?"

"Your feet."
I pull my knees up
and spread my toes on the braided rug.
"Well . . ."
One nail is black.
I didn't cut it short enough,
so the skin bruised underneath.
Three toes have open blisters.
The big callus on my right foot is really red.
"Yeah. I guess if I think about it, they hurt."
Grandpa's lips pinch into a line.
"It doesn't seem right."
"Grandpa, it's part
of learning ballet."
He shakes his head.
"All that dancing on your tiptoes.
Most people get arthritis when they're old.
But what will your feet feel like
after this much damage?"
I shrug.
He slips his feet out of his leather house shoes.
His nails are thick and yellowish.
His toes are knobby and bent like his hands.
"I ballroom danced, remember,
and you know I still love to ski.
But neither of those
equals the foot strain of ballet.
And now my feet hurt
on all our rainy days."

"Huh."

"I wish there was another way for you, Clare."

"Another way for what?"

"Well," he says as he slips his shoe back on,

"another way to dance

without damaging your feet."

"Yeah." I pick at some hanging blister skin.

"It would be great

if I could be a dancer

without this part."

I touch his shoe with my foot.

"But it's worth it."

The glass shelves
bounce the light
into my eyes.
I squint in the dark hall
and sip my water.
Army medals
rest on red velvet.
Old ski racing ribbons
line a whole shelf.
Most are first place.
A picture of Grandpa
dancing with Grandma.
Her gauzy turquoise dress floats
above the floor.
She was really beautiful.

Grandpa's treasures
are safe behind glass.
I flip off the light
and go to bed.

I kick my leg
as high as it can go.
Grands battements:
front,
side,
back,
side.
This is something
I can do with power.
Madame
presses her cold cane
against my hip.
"Control.
Control.
Control," she insists.
I have to lower my kick
so I don't jar
against her cane.
"Better." She walks past
tapping the rhythm.
But now
I'm only kicking
as high as everyone else,

and my grands battements
don't seem so special
anymore.

Rosella's on the other side of the barre.
The spot in front of me is empty.
It's Dia.
That's who's missing.
How can I miss Dia
when I didn't even know her?
But she was
one of us,
one of this class,
trying just as hard
as everyone else.
Now
there's an empty spot.

Elton
usually has to wipe the floor
during barre exercise.
He sweats so much.
His dark skin shines.
I need to sweat that much
to show I'm trying my best.
I'm going to work harder.

Today Tommy grips the barre
behind me.
I move up closer to Nathan.
I'll never feel comfortable around Tommy,
the way he flirts with all the other girls.
I don't like how his long hair clumps with sweat
by the end of the class.
Nathan's crew cut always looks neat.
So does Elton's short Afro.
I smooth my stray hairs back.
The pianist plays an intro,
and we sweep through the motions
Madame instructed.
Perfect synchrony
among near strangers.

Margot places one foot
on the little barre in the floor room
and slides.
A perfect split.

Rosella bends at the waist,
puts her hands
on the floor,
presses one heel
to the floor molding,
and runs her other leg
up the wall behind her.

A perfect split.

Elton sits facing the wall.
With his legs spread apart,
he scootches himself
closer and closer
until he touches
every inch of the inside of his legs
to the molding.
A perfect split.

I lie on my back
and lift one straight leg.
I pull it down against my chest
until my toes
touch the floor behind my head.
A perfect split.

Whatever way,
it has to be perfect.

Madame's sipping from her water bottle.
We have a couple more minutes to stretch.
"Isn't it weird she's gone?" I whisper to Rosella.
"What? Who?" She checks herself in the mirrors.
"You know. Dia."
"You're kidding."
"No, I feel like—"

"Oh please, Clare." She laughs.
"It's good she's gone.
She looked awful
with those big boobs
bouncing around.
She flopped all around the room.
It's good Madame took care of it.
We need the space,
and it was horrible to have to look at her.
Especially that big butt jiggling behind it all!"
What?!
Rosella tosses her towel on a chair.
"Come on," she says.
I don't move.
She keeps walking.

We bourrée—
little tiny steps
on pointe—
from one corner
to the other.
In one long line.
It's the worst time to see
how much I stick out.
My head is way above all the other girls.
My feet flick baby steps
almost as fast as my heart beats.

"Auditions will be held here, on Saturday.
10:00 A.M. sharp," says Madame.
She runs her cane through her fingertips.
"Students from
all over the Seattle-Tacoma area
will come to compete
for the sixteen City Ballet positions.
If you were a member last year,
you must audition again this year.
Nothing is guaranteed.
I expect your absolute best
as you represent the conservatory."
I'm amazed
her slick, tight bun
actually lets her smile.

I tug on my jeans.
"What you said
was pretty awful, Rosella."
"What?"
"About Dia."
"Oh, come on, Clare.
It's no big deal.
I only said what everyone's thinking."

I bend to get my stuff together.
The room feels more crowded than usual.
I'm bumping into rear ends,

elbows, and knees.

"I need to use the bathroom.
Wait to walk out with me, Clare."
I grab her arm. "You have to stop doing that."
"Clare, I have to pee."
"Oh, right."
"I do. What is with you today?"
She pulls away.

I step around a pile of clothes
and Margot changing her shoes on the floor.
I follow Rosella to the stall.
She does go.
But when she flushes
I hear her vomit.
I knew it.
This can't be right,
no matter what I was thinking before.
She's got to be losing strength.
It's dangerous.

Rosella comes out and crosses her arms.
"What?" she asks.
"I'm going to tell your mom
if you don't quit it."
"Big deal." She pushes by me.
"My mom's the one who tells me to do it.
Grow up."

She slips between the other girls
and disappears.

I stomp,
stomp,
stomp
around the window shoppers
looking into the gift stores.
The sidewalk is extra crowded.
I want to get away from everyone
and back to Grandpa's.
I should have cut through the alley.
Sure, my mom is like a cheerleader
about our dream,
and my dad says I can't fail,
but her mother
tells her
to vomit?

Rosella's mom has always
been into clothes
and cool cars.
Going through three husbands
and getting tons of alimony,
she is used to having whatever she wants.
Maybe Rosella has to be
the daughter that fits her style.

The perfectly thin ballerina
to accent her vogue life.
Vomiting
to make her mother happy.

It makes me
want to puke.

Grandpa pulls his little car
up to the curb.
"Come on, Clare."
I duck by the hanging basket and get in.
"Where are we going?"
"It's a nice day for a short hike."
"But Grandpa,
I haven't changed."
"You'll be fine."
He pulls out onto the street,
turns on Main,
and heads up toward the Cascade Mountains.
"But I need a snack."
"I packed some goodies.
Relax, Clare."
"But I'm wearing clogs."
"Your hiking boots and socks are in the trunk.
Before you know it,
ski season will be here,
and I want to be in shape for some downhill

on Crystal Mountain."
I shake my head.
Grandpa has skied
since forever.
It drives Mom nuts with worry.

I sink back against the seat
and watch the traffic disappear,
until we are alone on the road
weaving up into the foothills.
Grandpa flips on the radio.
I close my eyes,
shut Rosella out of my mind,
and choreograph a dance
to the classical music.

The gravel crunches.
Grandpa parks the car.
He gets my boots and socks,
and I pull them on.
"Ready." I grab the pack from the backseat
and hand him his walking stick.
We lock up.
"Here's the trail." He starts off
through the bushes.
I follow.
Ferns stretch over the path.
Sun shafts slice between the firs.

I breathe in the sweet
growing, decaying smell.
The moss is spongy under my feet.
Grandpa leads the way.
I follow.

"Wow. Look at those roots
on that fallen tree, Grandpa.
They must be twelve feet across."
"Looks like an old cedar."
The trail switches back,
and we walk the length of the downed tree.
"Sure the forest is beautiful.
But don't you think
this rotting tree is awesome too?"
Grandpa says, "Definitely."
He puts his arm
around my shoulder. "Look at all the life
that can grow on it now."
Moss, baby ferns, even a couple little trees
are springing from its side.
"Amazing," I whisper.

I pull back my tights
and dip my feet in the river.
"Ahhhh."
Grandpa laughs at me.

"What? It feels great!" I say.
"I'm sure." He gathers up our trash
and tucks it into the pack.
The water burbles around my ankles.
The cold prickles and needles my skin.
I yank my feet out.
Mmmmm.
The rock is warm,
and my wet footprints
evaporate in seconds.
A ladybug creeps onto my hand,
then flies off.
The alpine meadow rustles around us.
"Hear that?" asks Grandpa.
"The marmots?"
"We always called them whistling pigs."
I laugh.
The whistles drift away.
"So you're really getting ready
for ski season, Grandpa?"
"Wouldn't miss it for anything."
"But you'll wear the helmet Mom got you?"
"Yes, I will.
And no backcountry without a buddy."
"Great. That sounds a little safer."
"You can join me if you want," he jibes.
"Yeah, right.
You know I hate heights, cold, and speed."
"That about describes the entire ski experience."

"Exactly. The only time I like speed
is when I'm spinning on pointe."
"Fair is fair. You speed across the floor
on your tiptoes,
and I'll *shoosh* down the slopes."
"Deal." I grin.
He stretches and gets up.
"Time to go, Clare."
I pull on my socks and boots.
We hike down the dimming trail
side by side.

"Whoa!"
"Grandpa!" I catch his arm.
He regains his balance.
Little pebbles
tumble over the side of the hill.
He squeezes my hand. "Thanks, love."
"Sure. This switchback is steep."
"And I'm old. I'd actually
do better on a pair of skis."
"I bet!"
He gives me a shaky laugh
and grips his walking stick
for the next step.
I keep close by.

Grandpa steers the car
down the dark dirt road.
I tilt up his old Army canteen.
Nothing. "I'm so thirsty."
"I'm sorry I didn't bring more water.
I forget how much you drink after class."
"That's okay. Thanks for sharing yours."
"We should always bring tablets to purify
the river water."
"Yeah." I screw the cap back on.

We pass a deer crossing sign.
I suck in some air through my teeth.
"What?" asks Grandpa.
"Oh, the deer sign makes me nervous
that one is going to jump out in front of us."
"I'm watching. You help."

The car bumps along,
its headlights bouncing and jarring.
"There!" I yelp.

Grandpa slows the car.
A doe is running up the hill
away from the road.
She leaps gracefully
over the rocky ridge
and disappears in the dark.

"Beautiful," we say together.

Thousands of tiny ladybugs
pour out of my heart
and rush over my body.
I'm covered head to toe,
and they begin to glow.
I dance in front of the black sky
perfectly.
Faster and higher.
Spinning and jumping
until
my foot cramps.
The ladybugs turn black
and fall off,
clattering to the floor.
The sky shatters,
and shards crash to the earth.
I wake up.

Oh, man!
A charley horse!
The pain bites
and grinds the muscle in my arch
up into the bone.
The muscle
is twisting, trying to flip over.

I jump out of bed
and crash around the room.
Grandpa comes in.
"Put your weight on it," he says,
and loops his arm
around my waist.
"I can't!"
"Do it," he says.
"Ow, ow, ouch."
He helps me walk off the cramp.

There.

"How can it hurt so bad,
but when you finally stand on it,
it eases away with tingles?"
"It just does," he says.
"And why's it called a charley horse, Grandpa?"
"I've never heard."
"Me either."

I give him a hug
and notice
he feels so small.
My head is above his.

"Now get back in bed," he tells me,
"and I'll bring you some water.
You must be dehydrated.

I'm so sorry I didn't bring more water
for the hike."
"It's okay."

I crawl under the sheet
and rub my foot.
My toes aren't pulled apart
like a wishbone anymore.

Grandpa brings the water.
I gulp it down.
He slides both windows closed.
"Don't want you getting chilled.
Good night, love," he says.
"Good night, Grandpa."

Prunes again this morning.
I stare at the
bloated blobs
floating
in Grandpa's bowl.
He slurps them down.
I gobble up my low-fat breakfast bar.
My foot is a little sore
from the charley horse last night.
I massage it while I sit at the table.
"Thursday Bible study for me this morning,"
Grandpa says.

"Oh."
"We have such a good group,
and the study is very intriguing about—"
I zone out until I hear,
"You know you are welcome to come
and worship with me on Sundays."
"Yeah. But it's just not for me, Grandpa."
He straightens the place mat.
I'll tell him how I feel.
That's not talking back.
"Since Mom and Dad have never gone to church,
it would be really weird for me.
Remember we talked about it before?"
"Oh, yes. But I thought you might have
changed your mind."
I shake my head.
"Well, I guess I'll be going then," he says.
"Would you load the dishwasher?"
"Sure." I smile to make it up to him.
He pats me on the back.
"Have a good class."
"You too," I say.

I push the dishwasher closed.
I don't have to go to church,
and he's not going to make me
feel guilty or anything.
I wipe the counter with the sponge

and squeeze the water into the sink.
Not one bit of guilt in me, Grandpa.

Liar.

I avoid Rosella while she changes
and go early to the empty barre room.
I rest my ankle on the top rung
and slide it
until I'm in a split.
I close my eyes,
and the stretch warms the back of my thigh.
"Hi, Clare."
It's Elton.
"Hi." I pull back up.
He stretches on the other side of the barre.
His leg slides clear to the end.
"You ready for auditions?" he asks.
I shrug. "I'm a little nervous."
"You'll do great." He slides back up.
I bend at the waist and hug my head
to my knees to hide my blushing.
"Thanks," I finally answer,
and straighten.
"I was in City Ballet last year
with Margot," he says.
"I know."

"So, believe me.
You'll make it."
I smile back at him.
We reach for the barre
and brush hands,
his dark,
mine pale.
I quickly straighten my skirt.

Plié, down and up.
The guys in class
seem nice enough.
Especially to each other.
This must be one place they can make friends.
Kids at their schools must be brutal
when they find out
the guys take ballet lessons.
I'm sure a lot are hassled about being gay.

Plié, down and up.
Tommy's the only irritating guy here.
He's actually eyeing Devin again.

Plié, down and up.
Nathan seems really sweet.
He's driven and focused to get better.
But Elton is by far the best.

In ballet and friendliness.
Overall, the guys are like the girls,
in that we are all here to do the same thing.
To learn to dance.
Maybe because the competition isn't so intense
for them,
they can be more relaxed.
Could I make friends with one of them
sometime?

Plié, down and up.
"And turn," says Madame.

The rhythm of the music.
The rhythm of the traffic outside.
The rhythm of our feet
brushing the floor.
It feels good
to be in rhythm.

I wait behind Rosella
at the water fountain.
Her backbone pokes out each notch
like a row of tiny fists.
She wipes her lips and steps away.
"Hi," I say.
She barely nods,

then joins her group on the floor.
I bend over the fountain
and drink deeply.
The cold contracts my chest
into a knot.
I sputter out the mouthful
and step away.
It's my group's turn.
I take the spot Rosella stood in
a second ago.
There's still a twist
in my chest.

I shoulder my bag
and cross the street
to the coffee shop.
I wait in the noisy line
and order a cup of tea.
The other customers' chatter
and the latte machine's hissing
cover me up
while I sit at the little table.

So Rosella ignored me the whole time,
but it feels so good
that Elton believes I'll make it
into the company.
I squeeze

the honey bear
tight around the waist
and swirl the gold stream
into my cup.
That's a sweet thought.

"Hi," she says.
I don't breathe.
Dia sits down
across from me.
My wood stirrer
slips from my fingers
and sticks to the table.
"Hi," pops out of me.

She looks so different
in street clothes
with her hair
down loose.

"I was walking
by the conservatory
and saw you come in here."
"Oh," I say.
"So, how was class?"
"Normal."

We sit.

"Not like yesterday,
when Madame actually smiled," I add.
"No way!" says Dia.
Now we both smile.
It feels great.

"So, how are you?" I finally ask.
"I don't know. Okay?"
She bites her thumbnail.
"You know what she said to me?"
"What?" I lean forward.
Dia looks at the ceiling.
"She said
I don't have a dancer's body.
That I should
redirect my efforts.
That I would be welcome
in the adult class."
I gasp. "How humiliating!"
"Tell me about it.
Most of them are so lame,
they can hardly move across the floor."
"So, what are you going to do?"
Dia shrugs. "I guess I kind of knew
this was going to happen.
I started imagining it awhile ago."
"Yeah?"
"Mmm hmm. I had time to get used to the idea."

She tucks her bra strap back under her shirt.
"Mostly I'm going to hang out,
take it easy the rest of the summer.
Then maybe I'll try out for lacrosse."
"That'd be fun," I make myself say.
"Yeah. 'Cause there's no way I'd ever
go to that adult class.
What a bunch of losers."
"Right." I smooth my napkin.
"But won't you miss ballet?"
Dia flips her hair behind her shoulder.
"Maybe. But I'm ready to try other stuff.
I don't have
a choice."
She pulls her chair closer.
"You know one thing?" she asks.
"What?"
"I still felt beautiful
when I danced.
All the way up to the last class.
Maybe I didn't look that great,
but I felt like I did.
Way down
deep inside.
You know what I mean?"
"Maybe," I whisper.
Maybe that's another name
for being turned inside out.
Beautiful.

"Would you believe this is a
double tall mocha latte
with whole milk and whipped cream?"
"You are kidding." I laugh. "That's a sin!"
"It's delicious!" She takes a big sip.
"Well, I better go.
I'm meeting my mom at the used bookstore."
"I grew up in a bookstore," I say.
"What do you mean?"
"My parents own the In Print bookstore
in Tacoma."
"Cool." She stands and pushes her chair in.
I wrap my hands around my teacup.
"Dia?"
"Yeah?"
"What did your mom say
after you worked so hard,
and it cost all that money—oh, never mind.
It's none of my business. Sorry."
"No, it's okay." She flips her hair again.
"We had a super long cry,
then talked about stuff
I've supposedly learned.
That kind of thing.
She really understood."
"Oh."
"It helped a little.
I mean,
everything

doesn't feel completely wasted."
She stares out the window.
"Most of the time.
Well, I gotta go, Clare.
Good luck on Saturday."
"Thanks."
She pushes out the door.
I swallow the rest of my cool tea
and follow her.

I bet her mom
never used to say
dancing
was their dream.

"Bye," I call
to Dia and her mom
on the opposite street corner.
They wave back.
I turn away
and hurry to Grandpa's.
He shouldn't be home yet
from his Bible study.
But just in case,
I don't want to worry him,
since I didn't call
and leave a message about staying later.

Oh. Dia's phone number.
I should get it
and call her sometime.
I sprint back to the corner,
but they're gone.
I shiver in the warm sun.
Oh, well.
Maybe it would have been weird
to ask for her number.
But it does seem like
if we aren't in class
we can talk.
Outside the conservatory
we are on the same side.
We could be friends
or something.

I beat Grandpa home.
My stomach is too jumpy for a snack,
so I yank my covers up on the bed
and stretch out
with some magazines.
I flip through the pages of ballet pictures.
Everyone looks the same.
The corps dancers
are a unit.
They are like one dancer,

each holding the exact same pose.
Same hair,
costumes,
height.
Same, same, same.
I flip the page.
A close-up of a soloist.
I cover her nose and mouth with my thumb
and look at her eyes.
There's too much makeup
to see how she really feels.
Beautiful?
Happy?
Does she love to dance?
She must.
The pain
has to be worth it.

I toss the magazine
and pick up the teen one
I checked out at Grandpa's little library.
"Cleavage: How to Get It"
"Dramatic Eye Shadow"
"Does He Think You're Seventeen?"
I flip through to the end.
Total obsession with breast size.
Page after page of fashion.
How weird that most girls
want to look older

every way possible.
Wow. How different can you get?
They want big breasts.
They want cleavage
and want to show it.
Why does it matter so much?
Because that's what guys notice?
Please.
What a load of garbage.

I have the opposite pressure.
I need to stay flat.
Nothing can interrupt your line in ballet.
Like a C-cup size.
Poor Dia.
She definitely looked different
from everyone else.
But is that so bad?
Why do we all have to look
like we're eleven?
Most of the time,
we look like little boys
partnered with men.
Why does it have to be like that?
Is the line so important?

Why can't we be the way we are,
not how a magazine or dance company says?
Am I believing a load of garbage too?

My poster is curling up again.
I reach and press
the corner of Baryshnikov to the wall.
It sticks for a few seconds,
then pops up again.
"Stay." I push harder.
This time it does.
But for how long?
The sticky stuff isn't worth much.
Maybe some tape
right across the edge would work.
I'll get some later.

"Hello?"
"In the kitchen, Grandpa."
I take the bags of groceries from him.
"I was getting worried about you."
"I'm sorry. I needed to do some shopping."

He rummages through the medicine cupboard
and pulls down his pills.
I pack the freezer with our dinners.
He swallows his medicine
with some water.

"And I stopped at the clinic."
I shut the freezer. "Is everything okay?"

"Yes." He sets his empty glass in the sink.
"They wanted to check my blood pressure."
"Oh."
"And how is *your* blood pressure, love,
considering auditions are a day away?"
"All right. I haven't been very hungry though."
"Nerves."
"Yeah." I cram the grocery bags
into the recycle bin.
"Nerves."

I dump our microwave dinner dishes.
"Want to go for a walk, Grandpa?"
"I'm not really up for it, Clare."
"Okay. I guess I'll go to bed early then."
"Good night."
"Night."

I take a quick shower,
crack my windows for some fresh air,
and climb into bed.
The fir trees shush outside.
My mind is stuffed with
Rosella saying those awful things,
Elton saying such a sweet thing,
Dia saying she's ready to move on,
and my mom saying it's our dream.

Why hasn't that bothered me before?
Why now?
Have Dad and Grandpa
ever really used those words?
Nope.
Dad's always saying I won't fail if I try hard,
and Grandpa says I'm already a dancer.
Even though that bothers me,
it's not like what Mom says:
our dream.
It makes the pressure twice as much.
Ugh.
I cover my head with my pillow
and try to suffocate my mind.

Grandpa's note says he's off to the library.
SEE YOU LATER,
I write across the bottom.
I clean up the kitchen
and toss a load of whites in the washer.
I shove up my covers
so the bed looks mostly made.
Where's my bag?
There, under the dresser.
I grab it and hurry out the front door.
"Hey, Mija."
Her black fur warms my fingertips.
She stretches and purrs,

then curls back into a ball on the stair.
Mmm. I'd love to curl up in the sun.
My bag slips from my shoulder.
Class!
I hurry out of the garden
and race down the sidewalk.

Tension zings around
the dressing room.
Bobby pins are shoved into buns.
Elastic is snapped at the waist.
Bags are kicked under chairs.
If the tension
is this bad today,
what will it be like
tomorrow?

I tug my tights up.
Rosella tries to slip past,
thin as a garden snake.
"Rosella—"
"Hey, forget it."
"But—"
"We're fine,
if you stay off my back
about my weight.
Come on." She drags me
by the wrist to the barre room.

It wasn't about your weight, Rosella.
It was about puking
and how rude you were about Dia.
And I wasn't apologizing.
But if you want to think so,
I don't care.
I have enough to worry about.

"Can you believe auditions
are tomorrow?" she asks.
I shake my head.
Everyone is waiting for Madame.
Rosella and I
end up on opposite sides of the barre.

"Again."
"Higher."
"Faster."
"Control."
"Taller."
"Stretch."
"Lean."
"Reach."
"Bend."
Translation:
Be
better
than

you
are
or
you
will
be
nothing.

We grasp the barre
while we balance
on one foot.
One leg is bent and lifted
to the front.
I love holding the attitude pose.
Everyone is solid.
"And release the barre," says Madame.
We do
and stay balanced.
Rosella
and Tommy
drop out of form.
They mutter under their breath.
Then everyone else collapses.
Margot, Elton, and I
are left balancing.
Madame walks slowly around us
looking down her nose.
"Other side," she snaps.

We come down and turn.
Margot glances at me.
I risk a smile.
She doesn't return it.
But Elton winks.

The adult class
laughs and chats
as they head
to the dressing room.
Everyone
wears something different.
They're like a circus troupe.
We pass them
silently
and go into the floor room.
I'm last in line.
"Good luck tomorrow,"
someone says.
I turn and see
the red-headed lady
looking right at me.
"Thanks," I answer
by accident.
I spin away
fast.

We piqué turn across the floor.
Snapping our heads,
we spot
one speck
on the wall
we are moving toward.
The room blurs,
but the spot
is in focus.
Everyone moves
across the floor
toward their spot.

Waiting for my turn,
I look outside.
Mount Rainier is hidden today.
It's hard to believe it's really
still there.
Something so huge,
but you can't even see it.
Below, cars rush past
Hurrying to other places.
I take a deep breath.
I'm right where
I'm supposed to be.
Being the best I can be.
I can definitely see it.

We escape the dressing room
as fast as possible.
Rosella didn't even puke today.
She and I
run into Elton going out the front door.
He holds it open for us.
"Thanks," we say.
"Sure. See you tomorrow!"
"Okay." I grin.
Rosella yanks me down the stairs.
"Come on," she giggles. "Be cool, girl."
I hurry away with her
even though Elton is still waving.

"See you, Clare." Rosella climbs
into their car.
"Later," I call, and then walk home
the straightest way possible.
The crosswalk light is green.

Grandpa's widening the pansy bed.
"What do you think?" he asks.
"It'll be beautiful!"

I fix tomato soup and grilled cheese
for dinner
and don't burn the bread.

"It's ready, Grandpa," I call out the storm door.
"Go ahead without me, Clare.
I want to finish up out here."
"Okay."

I try to eat
but end up dumping nearly all of mine
since my stomach's crampy.
When Grandpa comes in,
he says his is delicious.

We play Scrabble till bedtime.
I win by two points.

I run the perfect temperature bath
and get out before it cools off.

I set my folded clean tights and leotard
on the dresser with my bag.

I check my toe shoes.
The boxing is a bit soft,
but the shank is still stiff.
Should be fine.
Everything is perfect
for tomorrow.

Willow

I think their little audition is today. I wouldn't know for sure; I lose track of time since my schedule is so packed with classes. City Ballet? Please. I'm mother's prima ballerina. She says New York is mine.

Rosella

I'm ready. I've done everything. New tights, new leotard, new shoes. I'm at my lowest weight. I will be one of the sixteen!

Dia

Today's the audition. I stuck my tongue out at the stupid kitchen calendar. So I'm childish. Who cares? What a relief I'm not under that audition pressure. Sheesh. Why did I ever want to dance anyway? Stop crying already!

Margot

Oh, right. The audition.

Elton

I am pumped for this audition. I lifted weights and drank a double protein drink this morning. Let me at those judges.

Clare

This is the dream I've sacrificed for. I've tried as hard as possible. Failure's not in my future. I'm going to go for that moment when

I feel turned inside out. I'll show everyone who I really am: the perfect choice for City Ballet Company.

My eyes are puffed
from not sleeping so well.
I tossed through the night,
visualizing every ballet step
I know.

Now I can't get my toast
to go down.
Or my orange juice, either.
My heart is fluttering double time.
I want to get this over with.
Please,
give me the chance
to dance.

Grandpa takes my face
in his hands.
His lilac aftershave is sweet.
"Remember," he says.
"I know. Do my best."
"No, Clare."
"What then?"
"Remember you are a dancer."

He kisses me on the forehead.
"We'll see," I say,
and pull away.
I can't take a long story or lecture
this morning.
I can't.

The front door clicks closed
behind me.
I hurry through the steady drizzle.
The clouds are so heavy
the morning is more like dusk.
The sidewalk's slippery with damp moss
that seems to have grown overnight.
At the intersection
I wait under a huge spruce tree
for the light to change.
The car lights reflecting on the asphalt
make the road look like a stage.
A semi truck honks,
and I hurry across
to the conservatory.

The dressing room is packed
with girls from all over the area.
Total strangers.
I don't see anyone yet

that I recognize.
Knees and elbows clash
for space to change.
I stash my stuff
and hurry out
so I don't have to fight
for air to breathe.

I step up to the registration table.
"Name?" asks the small woman
over her clipboard.
"Clare Moller."
Scratch, scratch.
"Slip this over your head
and tie the sides.
You're number one."
"One?" I gulp.
She grins.
I take the crinkly bib
and turn around.
No one else
has a number yet.
They're all stretching
at the barre.
I'm the fool
who registered first.
Now I'll be the first.
The first in every lineup.

The first for every combination.
The first to fail.

I move through the crowd
with my shoulders back
and my head up.
I can at least convince everyone
I wanted to be number one.

Squeezing the barre,
I bend and stretch,
covering my face
as much as possible.
Against my knees
or under an arm.
Any position to hide my eyes
threatening to spill tears.

There's Margot.
And Elton.
And Rosella.
Way in the back
with high numbers.
My heart bangs my ribs
like the pianist warming up the keys.
The same lady as usual at least.
One more face I know.

Or at least have seen a lot.
The last girls and guys drift
like numbered notes
to the barres.
I stand at the head
of the first group
and peek again
over my shoulder.
They are all shorter than me.
Every single one
but Elton.
I tug my bib straight
and face forward.

The judges line
the front of the room.
They're crouched behind a table
cluttered with notepads,
pencils, and water bottles.
Who knows who these people are?
Maybe teachers from PNB?
Oh, there's the one guy with the goatee
who teaches the adult class.
He must like judging
better than teaching that group.
But he looks grumpy,
like all the rest of them. Great.
Madame's tapping cane

brings my focus back.
She leads us through
our barre work
like it's an ordinary day.
For once,
looking at her
helps me to relax.
I turn all my thoughts
inward
and move like I've been trained.
It helps to have
a thick iron barre
to hold on to.

Tendue, point, and close.
I feel every bone in my left foot
brush the floor.

Tendue, point, and close.
A blister is growing
on my big toe.

Tendue, point, and close.
The callus
on the ball of my right foot
is burning hot.

Tendue, point, and close.
Still,
every bone moves exactly right.

The herd of us
moves down the hall,
following the judges
to the floor room.
We are moving through this narrow space,
but no one is touching.
A girl carrying her toe shoes
trips on her ribbons
right in front of me.
She stumbles
and goes down on one knee.
Crack.
Everyone bends away from her.
She gets up on her own
and hobbles forward.
Is she hurt?
She favors the knee
but makes it into the floor room.
Anything can take a person down
right before
success.
With extra care,
I put on my pointe shoes

and tuck the ribbons deep.

Madame walks Group One
through the tricky combination.
I mark it with my hands like usual,
but the floor feels shifty.
I'm out in the open with this small group,
rather than being supported
with my classmates close by.

Madame concludes.
Breathe in through my nose
and out through my mouth.
Again.
The old man pianist plays an intro.
His music immediately snaps me into place.
I'm braced on all sides of my body
by the rhythm.
I can do this
totally alone,
as long as I have the piano music.

So far so good.
I wipe down
and watch Margot's group
move through the complicated
combination.

She's definitely the best.
Her line is perfect
from her fingertips to her toes.
The judges have to see that.
Even the girl who cracked her knee
is moving well.
I saw her wrap it before she took the floor.
Where'd she get the bandage at the last minute?
Doesn't look like her knee's bothering her a bit.
Sweat drips into my eyes.
I rub the acidy burn away.

The judges' pencils
scratch along with
our quiet panting,
gritty shoe leather
brushing the wood floor,
and someone cracking their back.
I hand Rosella her towel.
"Thanks," she mouths.
I smile.

"Group One,"
calls a judge with fake eyelashes
that curl up to her brows.
Yuck.
I hurry out

to the floor
for my turn.
What will they each scratch
about me?

The fifteen guys are grouped together.
It's weird to see
so many in one place.
Tommy is doing well
despite all the new girls around.
Nathan nailed his tour en l'air,
spinning high in the air
and landing in the same spot
he started from.
But Elton moves to the music
like no one else.
Those judges have to see his power
and grace.
He loves what he's doing.
Absolutely.

We line up for grands jetés
across the room.
I twist to stretch my sides
and catch Elton giving me a thumbs-up.
I smile, turn back,
take a huge breath,

run, and take off
in the highest, clearest leap
I've ever done.
I'm flying across the room
like the deer I saw with Grandpa!
The judges have to notice.
I've left everyone else behind.
I'm turned inside out.
This is me!
Beautiful!

The girls in the second group
are like small twigs
twirling in the wind.

I feel a bit faint.
Must be the tension
and not enough water.

I get a sip at the fountain,
then slide down in a corner
and close my eyes.

Satin pointe shoes squeaking
on wood,
rapping,
clunking,
thudding

over the creaking floorboards.

I open my eyes and feel
the girls land hard,
even when it looks like
they haven't landed at all.

Rap, rap, thud.

I've heard through
the illusion.

We all take the floor
and bow to the judges,
and then to ourselves
in the mirror.

I danced in here.
I rocked this place.
No one is going to tell me different.

We rise.
"High-five, Rosella."
She smacks my palm. "Yes!"

It's over.
All the work

I've done for ten years
made me ready
for this audition.
And now it's over.
My dream is beginning.

We untie and unwind
our pointe shoes
the same way.
We fold in the heel
and wind the ribbons
around the shank.
Doing the same thing alike,
we are one dancer
scattered into pieces,
waiting to be put together
as the corps
of City Ballet Company.

That one girl
unwraps her knee
and there's a huge goose egg
sticking up.
She hops to the wall to balance.
Man. That's tough.

"Please wait in the barre room."
Madame rolls her cane between her palms.
"The judges will post the City members
in half an hour."

We flow out the door
and through the hall
like a real ballet corp.
Cameras flash
in the barre room,
and we pull apart.
Newspaper reporters
want interviews.
I move away to the window
as they speak to Rosella.
She doesn't seem to mind.
"R-O-S-E-L-L-A," she spells.

Each journalist has found someone
to interview.
I'm safe for now.
Introverted and left alone.
Just the way I like it.
But a little lonely.
Elton's talking to Tommy
and Margot.
How do they think they did?
I could go ask.
I start to make my way toward them,

but the reporters push me aside
and gather in a tight circle.
What's going on?
I get a look through their legs
at a girl on the floor
huddled in a ball,
crying.
"I'll never make it!" she bawls.
"I'm not good enough."
How humiliating!

"Clare."
I look up.
Madame is calling me
from the doorway.
"Would you join me in my office?"

I clasp my hands
to still the shaking.

"Sit down, Clare," says Madame.

I sit on the very edge of the chair.
My pelvis
nails the wood.

Madame slides into her seat
behind her big oak desk.

She opens a file.
My name is on the edge.

"Clare," she says.

My skin creeps.

"Clare, you are a fine dancer."

Yes!

"You are qualified
to be a member
of City Ballet Company."

I'm busting open,
my smile is so huge.
Tingles race
over my goosebumped skin.
"But . . ."

What?

"But . . ." She flicks through my paperwork.

The air whooshes out of me.
I'm like a paper doll
about to drift

off the chair.

"Your body is not well designed
for the ballet."
"But—"
"You are too tall,
and I speculate you haven't finished growing.
Clare, I hate for you
to devote yourself
at this level
to an art
you will never be suited for professionally."

The sweat on my back
freezes.

"But, Madame, I danced as well as anyone
at the audition."
"Yes, you did."
"I did really well."
"Yes."
"My développé was above hip level.
My, my—" My throat closes.

At least it stops my pathetic begging.

"Clare, I am sorry.
You *are* a dancer.

Which is why
I wanted to give you a chance at this audition
in case a taller group of girls turned out.
But it's not the case.
We have to face that you're not shaped
for classical ballet.
Before long
you'll be too tall
even for Pacific Northwest Ballet.
And in New York,
you would need to be a superstar
to succeed.
I don't see that potential in your work."

Breathe. Breathe. Breathe.

"I have to remove you
from your class, Clare.
The group is going to consist
only of City members now.
They will be dancing far more
with their additional commitment,
and you will be left behind.
Several other girls will be shifted
to alternate classes.
You in particular,
because of your height,
are welcome to join the adults."
"The adults?" I squeak.

"The adult class.
There you could continue to dance
for your own enjoyment."
"I need to go now, Madame," I whisper,
and stand.
"I am truly sorry, Clare."
She closes my file.

Everything inside me
wants out.
I retch into the toilet
again
and again
until nothing else comes up,
but my guts keep trying
to crawl out
of my throat.
I heave sharp air,
then wipe the last dribble of vomit
off my lips
with a wad of toilet paper
and flush.

Everything swirls away.

I passed people
when I ran from the office

to the bathroom.
The reporters were still in the barre room
with a bunch of girls.
The dressing room
was full too.
But I don't remember any faces.
I'm not coming out of this stall
till everyone is gone.

Someone actually knocks.
"Are you okay?" she asks,
but gives up when I don't answer.
"We made it! We made it! We made it!"
two girls yell.
"I completely blew it," says another.
"My father's going to kill me."

I sit on the cold toilet cover
and wait till all the excitement, disappointment,
rustlings, and zippers disappear.

Rosella never found me.
Did she look?
I lean against the wall
and taste my thick, sour tongue.
I can't stop shivering.

The stall door creaks
when I come out.
Everyone's gone
from the dressing room.
Shaking,
I pull on my jeans,
clogs,
gather my stuff,
and cram it into my bag.
I run out.
The barre room's empty.
At least I don't have to look
at anyone.
Rosella.
Or Elton.
I race out onto the wet street.
It's like the conservatory
vomits me
out of its belly.

It's still sprinkling.
I step off the curb.
A car screeches, honks,
and swerves around me.
I rush across the street.
I feel so dizzy
stumbling past the shops.

I breathe faster and faster.
Sidewalk squares shift.
I splash through puddles.
Lights pierce my eyes.
There's Grandpa's hedge,
the porch swing,
Grandpa asking me something.
I'm falling.
Darkness.
Finally.

Lying in the backseat.
I don't have my seatbelt on.
"It's okay, love," says Grandpa. "It's okay."

Grandpa helps me out of the car.
Wheelchair
squeaking.
Thermometer
beeping.
Blood pressure cuff
tightening.
Stretcher
zooming.
Rubber strip
squeezing.
Needle

jabbing.
IV
taped down
to the pale hairs
on my arm.

Dehydrated.
That's all.

Dehydrated.

I twirl the armband on my wrist
and stare at the needle
submerged in my skin
dripping clear liquid into me.

How embarrassing.

I can't even keep enough water down
so I don't faint,
let alone dance.

The ER corner's empty
except for a picture of Goofy in Disneyland
and the Space Needle taped to the wall.
Neither one is enough to distract me
from the IV
and the mysterious machines.

This must be the kids' cubicle.
The two curtains shift as someone walks by.

I shudder
and pull the warm blanket
to my chin.
The cold IV
is chilling me
inside out.

Grandpa comes in.
He tugs the drapes closed behind him.
"You gave me a scare, love."
I bite my lip.
He smoothes my stray hairs
back toward my squashed bun.
"It'll be all right."
I shake my head no.
Tears pop out.
"I'm sorry," I whisper.
"No harm done."
"I'm sorry."
"Clare, we only need to make sure
you drink more."
"I mean about not making the company."
"Sh. Stop. I know all about it.
Madame called me

right after the audition."

"Everyone knows
I'm not a dancer—"
"Yes you are, Clare."
My lips start blubbering.
Grandpa still
doesn't get it.

"I called your mom and dad."
"Oh, no," I groan.
"Clare, they needed to know."
I kick at the blanket,
which hurts my feet,
but I don't care.
Grandpa straightens it out.
"They are on their way home.
They'll make it back tomorrow."

Our dream's dead,
and it's all my fault.
I shut my eyes.

Drip, drip.
Grandpa holds my free hand.

"Owwwww!" yells a little boy.
"The stick went into his eye!"
squeals a woman.
The screams are right on the other side
of my curtain.
I watch a group of feet
shuffle beside gurney wheels
out of sight and earshot.
I loosen my grip on Grandpa.
His eyes are closed.
Is he praying for them?

Drip, drip.
"Here, suck on some ice," Grandpa tells me.

Next there's a man who's hurt his back
and can't walk.
"Please, please give me more pain killer,"
he begs.

Drip, drip.
"One more bag, Clare."
The nurse adjusts the flow.

A woman wails,
"My baby!"
She brushes my curtain open
racing down the hall.
Grandpa pulls it closed.

How can stupid dehydration
compare to this stuff?
So much pain!
Why doesn't the doctor tell me
to go home already?

Shame heats my skin.
Because,
deep down,
it feels like my dream dying
does compare to all of this.
It's as bad as poking out your eye,
or your back hurting,
or your baby getting taken away.
My dream was like a baby to me.

I'm totally selfish.
How sickening.

"I have to use the bathroom."
"Let me get the nurse, Clare."
Grandpa hurries off.

I sit up, swing my legs
over the side,
and the Goofy picture spins.

"Hold it there."

The nurse catches me.
"Now try."
I stand on wobbly ankles.
And I'm not even on pointe!
She pushes the IV stand
into the hall.
"Excellent," she says.
"Good job," says Grandpa.

Applause for walking
to the bathroom
wasn't what I was aiming for
today.

"And make sure she continues drinking.
Bye-bye, now."
The attendant waves
as Grandpa pulls the car away
into the night.
The dashboard clock says 8:26.
The day is gone.
The awful day
is over.

I swallow the last of the sports drink
and hand Grandpa the bottle.

"There, now. You rest, Clare.
I'll call and give your parents an update.
Before you know it
they'll be here."
I roll over.
He tucks the sheet.
"Call me if you need anything,"
he says from the doorway.
"Okay."
How about a new life?

In my dream,
I'm dancing alone
on a stage
when things start turning to paper.
The backdrop,
curtains, and floor
ruffle in the wind,
then tear apart and spin away
into the air.
"From the top," Madame's voice
blares over an intercom.
"From the top."
But there's no place left
to dance.
A last gust tips me over
and wafts me through the emptiness.

The sun creeps under
the edge of my blind
and spears my eyelid.
I squint.
My ballet bag
is sitting on my dresser.
A toe shoe pokes out of the opening.
I fling my pillow across the room.
It hits the dresser mirror, which
knocks my bag to the floor.
Clud, thud.
I sit up and stare at myself.
I'm pale.
Bobby pins dangle
in my hair,
out of place and useless.
I yank them out,
deserving the pain.

"I don't see that potential
in your work," she said.
I'm not good enough
to be a superstar.
Not
good
enough.
Not only too tall.
I didn't try hard enough.

I tilt the mirror down
so I don't have
to look
at myself.

"There you are, love."
I sit at the kitchen table.
Shivers spread across my back.
Grandpa reaches over
and rubs my arm.
The heat from his firm hand feels good.
"It's almost noon.
How about some green tea?" he asks.
"Sure."
He gets up and pours the hot water
into a mug with a bag.
"I was expecting you
to be up and around soon." He smiles,
passes me the tea
and the honey bear.
I warm my hands around the mug.
The bear shimmies when I try to squeeze him.
"Let me help you." Grandpa gets the honey out.
I stir it and take a sip.
"We have to double up on your drinking today."
"Yeah."
"Otherwise, you'll be back in the hospital
before you know it."

"I'll try to drink a lot, Grandpa."
"I can always count on you to try, Clare."

I kick the dance bag
out of sight under the dresser
and pull on shorts and a T-shirt.
Hey, it's Sunday.
Grandpa gave up church this morning.
One more sacrifice for me.
Maybe he can still go tonight.
I yank the brush through my hair.
So many tangles.
This is a rat's nest, Mom would say.
I pull harder to get the bristles through.
My hand slips and bangs on the edge of the dresser.
Ow!
I rub the red spot,
then pull my hair into a ponytail
without finishing.
All the tangled knots are lumpy.
Who cares?

I nudge the porch swing with my toe.
The cool afternoon air
nudges me back.
Maybe a summer storm is moving in?
That can make the temperature drop fast.

Mija leaps up
and curls in my lap on the blanket
Grandpa made me bring out.

How long till the blisters on my feet heal?
How long till, "You aren't fit for ballet,"
stops chanting in my head.
I pet Mija's fur
backward.
She purrs.
How long till Mom and Dad get here?
What will I say?
At least I didn't have to talk to them
this morning.
Grandpa told them it'd be better to chat
when they got here.
Definitely.
I wish I could get out of it then too.

I pick the newspaper up off the swing
and pull it out of the plastic.
I flip through the sections.
I'm sure it's in here.
Do I want to look?
My hands keep searching.
Entertainment.
My stomach flips.
I open the section.

"City Ballet Selected."
My hands sweat and stick
to the newsprint.
I scan down the list.
Rosella.
Elton.
Margot.
Ellen.
Devin.
Nathan.
Tommy.
I recognize names of other kids in my class.
Of course they'd almost all make it.
The conservatory is the best instruction
in western Washington.
Back to the list.
No Clare.
I rub the list of last names starting with M.
Mine doesn't appear.
The ink smears.
I let out a big shaky breath.
The picture is of that girl
on the floor crying.
I feel a chill
and turn the page to see the rest of the report.
"No. No!"
There's a photo of everyone gathered around
the posted list.
And one girl in the background is running

to the dressing room.
One girl holding her stomach.
Me.

Grandpa's still inside.
I cram the section of the paper
into the trashcan
and cover it with other bits of garbage.
Damp, cold coffee grounds,
limp tea bags,
tomato slime,
wadded tissues.
I put the lid back on,
and the metal rattles
like my bones are shaking.
I drag my hands on the grass
till all the ick comes off.
No one is going to see that picture.
Except
the rest of the city.

"Clare!"
Mom jumps out of the car
before Dad completely stops.
She rushes over to me.
I set Mija aside
and get up too quickly from the swing.

My eyes see spots and I fight the dizziness.
She pulls me close in a hug
and my head clears.
"Oh, sweetheart. Are you okay?
How are you feeling?
Are you alright?"
"Yeah," I answer.
"There's my girl!" Dad steps up,
and it's a group hug.
At least this way
I don't have to look them
in the face.
And Dad didn't say,
"There's
my failure."

"There, now." Dad gets me settled
on the swing.
It's so good to see him.
We haven't talked on the phone lately.
He drapes the blanket over my legs.
Mom hovers behind him.
I can't see anything but her little feet
because he's so tall.
Why did I end up like him?
Why?
He squeezes my shoulder.
"Are you comfortable, Clare?"

"Yeah." I smile
and clench my teeth
to keep
my bubbling anger
in.
It's not his fault
I'm huge.
Really, it's not.
Besides,
he's my dad!

"I'm sorry you guys
had to leave your convention early."
"Clare. Don't even bother to think about it,"
says Mom.
"Not another thought."
"Exactly," Dad agrees. "You
are what's important to us."
Grandpa brings out biscotti
and fresh coffee on the teacart.
Mom pulls her chair closer to the swing.
"Now, are you sure she's okay, Dad?
Is that what the doctor said?"
"If she keeps drinking, she'll be fine."
Grandpa passes a cup to my father.
He takes a sip. "Well, she looks great to me."
I smile and drain my water bottle.
"Let me get you more.

I'll be right back." Mom hurries inside.
The storm door bangs behind her.
Dad shakes his head.
"She's really wound up, Clare."
"That's Mom."
"True."
Grandpa crunches the dry biscotti.
Little crumbs tumble down his shirt front.
He doesn't brush them off.
"Here you go," says Mom.
She stands over me until I drink.
"Everything, every little thing,
is going to be fine now," she says.

"Inside," Mom announces. "I don't want you
getting chilled."
"But it will keep getting warmer
till 2:00,
the hottest hour of summer."
"She's right, Martha," says Dad.
"Yes, she is." Grandpa pours himself more coffee.
"Well, I heard a storm may blow in,
so it may not warm up at all," Mom argues.
I roll my eyes at Grandpa.
He shrugs.
"Inside, Clare," she says,
putting an arm around me
and pulling me up.

Life with Mom
is back.

She stares at the snarls
in my hair.
"This is a rat's nest."
"I know." I flinch.
"I'm sorry. It's going to hurt, honey."
"That's okay."
I watch her in the dresser mirror.
She's biting her lip,
and her forehead is bunched
into tight little lines
between her eyebrows.
She tugs the brush
through my hair.
"Your grandpa told us
about the audition."
I close my eyes.
She brushes some more.
"I'm sorry, Clare.
Let's talk about it.
Get it out into the open."
"No," I whisper.
She hits a huge knot.
I squeeze the tears in.
She's not touching me.
I look.

Mom's staring at my dance bag
peeking out from under the dresser.
A ribbon is under my foot.
"I'm sorry, Mom."
She puts her cheek
on the top of my head
and cries.
"We tried so hard," she says.

"Mom, can we talk about it later?
I need to rest."
"But don't you want to discuss
exactly what happened?
Who did what,
and how it felt to audition?
What everyone else said and did?
Your time in the hospital?"
I lift an eyebrow.
"All right, I can wait.
We have time.
And you are regaining your strength."
She sets the brush down
and wipes her eyes
on the back of her hand.
"We can talk later. Plenty of time.
Plenty." She tries to smile.
I climb back into my unmade bed.
She pulls the covers up.

"There. You rest now.
Get some deep relaxing rest."
"Okay."
She drops the blinds.
"Hear that rain?
I knew it was going to blow in.
That air was very cool—"
She shuts the door and cuts herself off.

"What will we do now?"
my mom asks.
"There's not anything for *us*
to do, Martha."
Dad's voice is a little harsh.
I lean against the bathroom door
and listen to them talk
in the living room.
"It's just that we've worked so long.
So hard.
So many lessons.
The hours and hours we've invested.
Clare has such potential, Dwight."
"And Clare has potential
for other areas.
Give it a rest, Martha.
For once in her life."
I flush the toilet
and go back to my room.

I work on my hair.
Slowly
I untangle every single knot.
By myself.
The brush runs smoothly
from the roots
to the ends.
I weave a clean, tight braid
and toss it over my shoulder.

After Grandpa gets back from church,
we sit down to dinner.
He helps himself to more bratwurst.
"This meal is lovely, Martha."
"Thank you, Dad. I'm glad you like it."
"I do too, dear," my dad says.
Mom smiles
but picks at her sauerkraut.
I actually
don't have to think about calories
or fat.
I can smash my face
into the bowl of mashed potatoes
if I want
and suck up the whole thing.

"Have you heard from Rosella, Clare?"
Mom asks.

I chew my bouncy bratwurst
longer than I need to.
"Um. No. I think she's probably busy
and stuff."
"What do you mean?
You've always been such good friends.
Didn't you call and tell her about
your trip to the hospital?"
"No." I scoop a big bite of sauerkraut.
It shocks my mouth,
and I squint.

"But I don't understand, Clare."
Mom sets down her fork.
I swallow the sour lump.
"Mom, she made it into the company.
She's not going to want to be friends
since I didn't."
"Oh, Rosella wouldn't act like that.
She's a dear.
You've known each other since preschool.
Maybe you are the one
who needs a little time
to deal with everything."
"Let's all take a little time," says Dad.
A picture of Dia comes to mind.
And I hear Rosella's voice saying, "Pathetic."

I don't need time.

It's not me who has the issue.

I curl up on the couch.
"Want any popcorn, Clare?"
Grandpa holds the bowl out to me.
"No, thanks." I rub my stomach.
"Dinner still doesn't feel so great."
"That was a rough menu
when you haven't eaten much
for a bit."
"Yeah." My belly rumbles.
"But it's the only thing that I thought of
when Mom asked what I wanted."
Grandpa flicks on the TV.
"They sure went to bed early," I say.
He doesn't answer.
"Grandpa?"
He stares at the TV, but his eyes seem focused
above the picture.
"Grandpa?"
"Yes?" He looks at me.
"They went to bed early, didn't they?"
"Oh, yes. Your dad's tired after the drive."
"Right."
He eats some popcorn.
"And he dragged your mother
with him. I'm guessing he's making sure
you have some space."

"Oh."
"I promised Martha you'd drink water,
and I'd tuck you in." He sighs.
"She's my girl,
but even I have to say
your mother beats the horse dead,
buries it,
digs it up,
and beats it again.
Like her mother used to."
I giggle.
"She's going to want to dissect
every inch of your experience, love."
"You're right."
I tuck my arm under my head.
Thanks, Dad.

I slide my hand over the phone.
It would be great to talk to Rosella.
If she wasn't in the company either,
we'd be bellyaching.
Digging into a tub of ice cream.
Making plans of what to do now.
Together.

Maybe she'll call.
Rosella?
No way.

In the morning
I wander through Grandpa's garden
and bend down to see the pansies.
When I stand up,
I'm not dizzy at all.
I'm definitely stronger today.
I rub the lamb's ear leaves
between my fingers.
The fuzzy softness
is comforting,
like petting Mija.
Dad's whistling
floats out of the house,
and my feet shift,
until my mind remembers
and cuts the glissade off
before one foot leaves the soil.
I'm not a dancer.
I go inside the house.

Mom gathers her purse and briefcase.
"I'll wait in the car for you, Martha," says Dad.
He gives me a kiss on the forehead.
"You call if you need anything.
Anything, Clare," he whispers.
I give him a hug.
My face brushes his rough cheek.
"You didn't shave," I say.

"I'm on it." He whips out his electric razor
from the overflowing book bag
he carries everywhere
and heads outside.

Mom turns to Grandpa. "So,
we've decided to stay with you
the rest of the week,
and then we'll leave on Saturday morning.
Dwight and I have our luggage
from the convention.
Clare will have time
to pack all of her things.
And well,
you know,
I can help out
around here a bit.
Cooking and such.
Then the three of us will head home.
Not that it's far.
It's just nice to be with each other for a few days.
While we all adjust.
A little vacation.
Don't you think?"
He stares at Mom and doesn't answer.
"Dad?"
"Oh, yes. Yes. Saturday, then."
"Clare, I've got to get going.
Your father is waiting.

Be sure to drink water,
have a healthy lunch,
and take it easy.
Remember,
you still owe me that chat.
There's so much to talk about."
"Uh huh."
"Okay. We'll be done with work around five."
"Fine. Fine." Grandpa walks her to the door.

Wow. Home on Saturday.
I didn't expect to go home.
I didn't expect not to make the company.
I didn't expect not to live with Grandpa.
I hate the unexpected.

"Here. Don't get up." Grandpa
moves the wheelbarrow closer.
"Thanks." I drop the dandelions in.
He bends down next to me
and tugs at a huge weed.
"There is an alternative
to you going home Saturday, Clare.
You have a choice."
"What?"
The weed gives, and Grandpa shakes the dirt
out of its roots. "You could stay here
and take the adult class the rest of the summer."

"Grandpa."
I yank some chickweed.
"I would never do that."
"Why?"
"That class is so lame."
He stares at me.
I go on. "You know.
None of them are ever going to be professionals.
They don't even work on pointe.
What is
the point?"
"Well." He tosses the weed into the barrow.
"Maybe
they like to dance.
Maybe
they are dancers."
I wipe my sniffle on my shoulder
and rip out some clover.
The weak leaves tear so easily
I almost fall backward.
Grandpa leans against me
till I get my balance.
"Take it easy, love."
I crawl away
and yank
more weeds.

"I'm going to grab a quick shower," says Dad.

"I was in the dusty storeroom all day."
"Okay, dear." Mom watches him
leave the table.
As soon as the bedroom door closes,
she turns to me.
"Clare, why don't we go for a walk
before it gets dark?"
Grandpa stands up.
"I'll do the dishes, but only if Clare
really wants to go."
I shrug. "Okay." Might as well get this over with.
Mom gets a sweater.
"Don't you need yours, too, Clare?
It's getting chilly."
"No. I'm fine."

"Mm, it's gorgeous," she says in the garden.
"It's that pink glow in the air."
"Yeah." I pause to pet Mija,
then we walk out to the sidewalk.
I take big strides,
and she double times it to keep up.
I'm not going to make this easy for her,
since she's not making it easy for me.

In the park we sit on the swings.
The place is deserted.
Getting dark.

The great old maple trees
look like they are up on their toes.
Their roots coil high out of the ground
rising to their massive trunks.
I used to love walking around the trees
when I was little and we'd visit Grandpa.
Up on their high roots,
I'd grip the spaces and pose
like I was doing a pas de deux.
"Oh, look.
Even Mount Rainier is pink." Mom points.
"It's beautiful."
"I hope you aren't too chilly," she says.
"I'm fine."
"I want to talk
about everything with you, Clare."

I let out a big sigh.

"Were you frightened in the hospital?"
"It wasn't that bad.
An IV and stuff.
More embarrassing than anything."

"I'm sorry I wasn't there for you, Clare."
"It wasn't a big deal, Mom."
"Well, then . . ."

She's not done.

Here it comes.
I grip the swing chains.

"I'm so sorry
we didn't make it into the company, Clare.
This has been our dream for so long.
Tell me everything.
What exactly happened?
Then maybe I can fix it for you."

Is she serious?
Fix it?
Fix the fact that I'm tall
and will never be
a professional ballet dancer?

She gives me a pathetic smile.
"Come on, honey.
Let it flow.
This was our dream.
You and me together.
Like always."

I'm sitting there
next to my mom,
and I'm hearing her say it:
our dream.
I'm not going to take it
anymore,

ever again.
She's not Grandpa.
I'm talking back.
She deserves it.
Now.

I rattle the chains with a jerk.
"What are you talking about, Mom?"

"I'm saying we're both devastated
because this has been our dream
for so long."

I jump up and shove my feet
into the bark chips in front of her.
I grind my fists into my hips.
"Mom!"

She stops her swing
to keep from bashing into me.

My chest is shaking.
"Dancing was *my* dream.
Not yours.
Mine."
My voice gets louder.
"I'm the one that worked for ten years.
I'm the one who pulled muscles,

whose feet
are disgusting.
I'm the one who didn't try hard enough.
I'm the one who dreamed.
I'm the one that grew too tall.
I'm the one
devastated."

I'm yelling now.

"I'm the failure.
This isn't about you.
This is mine!
Stop saying it's ours!
It never has been!
And you
can't fix it!"
I kick bark onto her shoes and run.

I scream
back over my shoulder,
"I'm not we!
I'm me!"

I run faster.
She can't catch up.

She should have

her own dreams.
She could have
been a dancer.
She's got the
short body.
But she didn't
go for it.
So that was
her choice,
and
she didn't
take it.
But I did.
Me.
Ballet
was
mine.

My sneakers pound the sidewalk,
and my feet sting.
I barrel into Grandpa's house,
straight to my dark room.
I slam the door,
slide down in the corner,
and pull my knees to my chest.

I'm a separate person
from her.

I failed.
But I did it
alone.
Let me at least
have that.

"Clare? There you are."
Mom comes in and shuts the door.
Her outline is barely visible.
The bed creaks.
"I . . ." She stops. "I don't understand."

Her shadow shifts.
"I don't understand your anger.
The way you were speaking to me.
Anything you said.
I always thought
of dancing as *our* dream,
Clare,
because I love you so much.
I wanted to work for the dream
with you."

I turn my face to the wall.

"I thought
driving you to lessons,
paying for them,

the shoes,
the tights,
the skirts,
the costumes,
the tiaras,
the soaking salts,
bandages,
toe caps,
every single bobby pin,
made it *my* dream too."

The bed sheets rustle
as she squirms.

"It was my dream, Clare.
Mine for you.
Ours."
"Shut up!" I whisper. "Just shut up, Mom."
"Don't you speak to me that way,
Clare!
You get control right now!
Do you hear me?"

My body trembles reaching
for a calm voice.
"I
did
it.
Yeah, you paid for it all.

But
I
sacrificed
myself.
And now we find out
I
did it
for
nothing.
But
it was
me."

Knock, knock.
"Not now," Mom and I yell together.
"Clare? Martha?" It's Dad.
I gulp.
"It's okay, Dad."
"You sure?"
"Yeah."

"Call me
if either of you
need me."
"Okay," we say.

"I can't believe

you are doing this to me, Clare."
Mom starts crying.
"This *was* mine, too.
I wanted it."

"For me or yourself?" I hiss.

"For you," she sobs.
I turn to her dark shape.

"What do I have
if it wasn't my dream?
What, Clare?
Nothing.
I have nothing without this."

"Maybe you've never had
anything, then, Mom."

"No, I did.
I had this dream for you."

"For me?
Prove it.
Say dancing was my dream.
Say it."

"Dancing was . . ."

"See? You can't even do that for me.

You want to fix this, Mom?
Admit dancing was mine."

I blow out air
and lean back against the wall.
She's hopeless.

She's so wrapped up in what I do
she can't separate herself.
She is
as bad as Willow's mother.
Who is
my mom?
It's like she wants to be me,
or us,
not herself.
What kind of weird psycho head game
is this?

She keeps crying.
Mumbling.
I sit there.

My clock flips by
sixteen minutes.
Long ones.

"Dancing

was . . .
your dream . . .
Clare,"
Mom sputters.
She crumbles to her knees
and crawls over to me.
"I'm so sorry, honey," she cries.

"For real, Mom?"
She hugs me tightly.

I let her,

then hug her back
a little.

"Your dream,
your dream," Mom keeps whispering
in my ear.
Rocking me back and forth.
"I did do nothing.
But watch
and root
and pay.
You are the one
who worked as hard as possible.
You
are

the dancer, Clare.
Not me."

Well,
not a dancer.
But it sounds like she heard me.
Un-be-lievable.

She lets go,
gets up,
and flicks on the light.
We blink hard,
look down and away
from each other.
We sit on opposite ends
of my bed.

"Really, Mom?"
She nods.
"You get it?"
"Yes."
"But why all of a sudden—"
"I'm your mother.
You're my baby.
It's taken your entire life
for me to see you separately.
I always knew you were independent,
but never faced

that you are an individual.

Till tonight. It's so hard, Clare.
Maybe you'll understand
if you have a child.
The drive is incredibly strong
to keep your baby
tight and close
so she stays a part of you.
How she started out."

Big tears run down her face,
but she doesn't wipe them off.
"It's hard to understand.
Isn't it?" she says.
"Yeah."

It's like we survived a tornado.
Everything feels blown to pieces,
but there's peace.
Quiet peace
between me
and my mom.

"Now that that is over,
and a long time coming, I imagine,

you have to promise to
tell me
about this kind of thing
sooner, Clare."
Oh, fun.
"So then,
can you please
tell me about the audition, honey?"
"Ugh!"
She's incredible.
Right back to the dead horse.
"Mom," I whine.
"No, I really want to hear.
I missed out.
I want to know what you went through
every second."
"Why?"
"Because I love you, Clare."
No answer to that.
So, after dragging out the stall
as long as possible,
I tell her how the audition went,
step by step.
She listens,
and glows with the excitement
and moans at the end
when I'm puking
after talking to Madame.
She listens to everything

about the hospital, too.

I can't believe it.
This is like talking to Rosella.
My mom wants every detail,
and she really does root for me
every second.
And there's no competition between us.
Weird.
Knock.
Dad opens the door and looks in.
Grandpa is peeking over his arm.
"Everything okay in here, ladies?" asks Dad.
"Fine," I say.
"Are you behaving yourself, Martha?" Grandpa
pushes into the room.
"Dad!" says Mom.
"Can I take that as a yes, then?"
She throws a pillow at him.
He catches it,
tosses it back to me,
and rubs his hands together.
"Well, how about some ice cream, then?"
"Yeah, how about it?" Dad grins.
"We'll be right there," says Mom.
The four of us look at each other.
It's so intense,
the feeling of okay,
I get goosebumps.

Mom's right there
to rub my arms.

I wash off my face
in the bathroom.
Is it for real?
Does Mom really believe
dancing was my dream?
That I'm a separate person?
How do you ever know
what someone's
thinking deep down?
They
might not even know.
Maybe she only wants
her peaceful,
everyone-happy
family.
So,
is it for real?

I can kind of see,
in a little tiny way,
she had a dream
for me.
Her dream
was that my dream

would come true.
Neither of ours
did.

At the table
we dig into our French vanilla ice cream.
Dad gave me a couple of giant scoops.
"So, what do you want to do now, Clare?"
Mom asks.
"Martha," Dad and Grandpa say.
"What?"
"It's okay." I let the coolness slip down my throat
before I go on.
"I don't know."
Grandpa looks over the top of his glasses at me.
"Madame told me Clare is a dancer.
She told Clare that herself."
"Huh. I really don't remember that."
I take another big bite. "It's strange now."
"How?" asks Dad.
"Well,
it's like I don't even know who I am
without ballet lessons."
Our spoons clink in the bowls.
"We've—" Mom starts.

I look at her.

"You've
done it so long,
I can see why." She scoops her last bite
and swallows it.
"It's going to be hard
to separate yourself
from ballet, Clare.
It's what you've always done."
I shrug and lick my spoon clean.
She sticks out her tongue
and licks her bowl spotless.
Grandpa and Dad do too.
I crack up.
Sometimes the unexpected
makes you laugh.

The guys tidy up the kitchen.
Mom leans her elbows on the table.
"Maybe I took your dream, Clare,
because I never had one of my own,"
she whispers.
She gets up and goes to the kitchen
before I can say
anything.

Get to sleep.

I flip over.
Not fit for classical ballet
is what I remember Madame saying.
Not good enough for New York.

Go to sleep.

I turn over.
Not have lessons
ever again?

Sleep!

I tug at the twisted sheets.
What am I
if I don't take ballet classes?
Who am I?
If I don't learn to dance,
will another dream come?
Do I want another?

Maybe it's like falling asleep.
You can't make yourself do it,
but it happens.

And then
you dream.

"Clare."
Someone's shaking my arm.

"Clare." Dad sits on the edge
of my bed.
"What?" I sit up. "What's wrong?"
"I'm sorry to wake you,
but your mother said
you called yourself a failure tonight."

"Uh, yeah.
City Ballet, Dad?"
"Clare, whenever I said
failure's not in your future,
I didn't mean
not getting what you want
makes you a failure."

I rub my eyes. "What?"

"I meant as long as you're trying,
you're succeeding.
If someone else says you don't make
City Ballet,
that doesn't mean
you're a failure."

Did Dia's mom try this one on her?

"All that hard work will yield something,
even if
it's not what you expected."

I scoot down under my sheets.
"I don't know, Dad.
I should have tried more."

"That's not what this was about.
It was about your height, Clare.
You can't control that."

"I wish."

"There's so little we can control, Clare.
The best we can do
is accept the situation,
learn from it,
and go on.
I mean it."

"Dad, can I go back to sleep?"
"All right." He kisses my forehead.
"But think about what I said. Okay?"
"Sure."

Did he make all that stuff up
so I wouldn't feel so bad?

But if I had tried harder
I could have been a superstar,
and my stupid height
wouldn't have mattered.

I squint in the dark
and pull the sheet to my nose.

Face it.
I tried as hard as I could.
I don't have
enough talent
inside me.

Mija
jumps onto
my bed
and curls
against
my neck.
I hiccup
into her old warm fur,
until
I fall
back
to sleep.

I follow Grandpa to the front door.
"Your folks said they'd be back around 5:00.
What are your plans today, Clare?"
"I'm going to walk down to the used bookstore.
I thought it would be nice
to get lost in a good, thick fantasy."
"Excellent idea."
"Don't tell Dad.
He always says he can get whatever book I want.
But it's fun to find something on my own."
"Understandable."
Grandpa gets his walking stick and a book. "You
want to meet for tea
at the coffee shop at 3:00?"
"Sure. I'll meet you there."
"Perfect." He opens the front door.
"You going for a hike, Grandpa?"
"No. A walk on the trail
around Bonney Lake after my book club."
"Have fun."
"You too." He kisses my cheek
and pulls the door closed behind him.

In A Good Book used bookstore,
I sit on my knees and
pull an old dance magazine
from the bottom of the pile.

This thing is ancient,
with Deirdre Carberry on the cover.
I promised myself I'd come in here
to get a fantasy novel to read.
But I can at least
look
at the dance magazines.
I flip through the pages
and Carberry performs a pas de deux
with Baryshnikov
from one picture to the next.
Perfectly.
Before I know it,
I'm bawling.
It feels like my ribs
are squeezing so tight,
my heart is going to be punctured.
I hold the magazine to my chest
and lean against the cold metal rack.
I cry and sway
without a sound.
I'm turned inside out
and there's nothing there
to show.

Keeping my face down,
I step up to the counter

with my book
and dance magazine.
At least this place is empty.
Maybe no one saw me losing it.
I smooth out the book cover
and clunk my money down.
"Clare?"
Elton's walking toward me
behind the counter!
"What are you doing here?" I ask.
"It's my summer job."
"Cool," I answer. "My parents own
the In Print bookstore."
"Now *that's* cool."
I smile, then remember
how absolutely embarrassed I am
about my life.
It gushes to my face.
I look down.
"Sorry about you not making the company,"
Elton says.
"I thought for sure you would."
"Thanks," I mumble. "Congratulations
for making it."
"Thanks."
He rings up my total on the cash register
and takes my money.
"I waited around for you, Clare,

after the audition,
to talk to you about it.
But I never saw you."
"Yeah, it took me awhile
to, you know,
get it together."
"Sure."
He hands me my change.
His warm palm
brushes against my weak hand.
I pick up my stuff
and turn to go.
"Do you want a bag?"
"Um, no thanks."
"Don't stop, Clare," he says.
"What?" I turn back.
"Don't stop dancing."
"But Madame kicked me out of class."
"It doesn't matter. You're a dancer."
I stare at him.
"Take the adult class," he says.
"It's not bad, sometimes I—"
"Why would I ever?"
"Because you love to dance."
I hurry out the door.

Elton
gets me all jumbled up.

But I can't keep from smiling.
That's really nice
that he'd still talk to me
even though I didn't make the company.
He was always different
from everyone else in class.

The clock on the bank says 2:15.
I can stop at the park
for a while.
I walk down the block
and refuse to look over at the conservatory.
I bet it's the little preschool class working now.
Learning their positions.
Stopping in front of the portraits of Madame.
Dreaming about wearing tutus.
Daydreaming—
yikes! Like me.
I start walking again.
And leave the conservatory
behind.

The magazine says
Deirdre studied dance in Miami, Florida,
in the 1970s.
Before she went to New York and danced with ABT

and Baryshnikov.
I bet the Miami school is like our
conservatory.
Wow. Willow could really make it
like Deirdre did.
She could be the one
to catch her dream.
If her mom doesn't get in the way.
You go, girl.

I stretch out my legs in the grass.
The maple moves shade on and off my magazine.
This edition is so old,
I bet most of these people aren't dancing on stage
anymore.
Even when you do make it to the top,
ballet is a short career.

Kids are swarming the playground area.
"Got you!
You're it!"
"Mommy, look at me!"
calls a little girl from the top of the monkey bars.
Her mom stands below.
"My, aren't we good climbers?"

No,
she is.

The little girl who did the climbing
is the good climber.
Not you, lady.
It's definitely a disease of motherhood.

I get up and go over to the woman.
"She's
a good climber," I say, and walk away.

The coffee shop is nearly empty.
3:30 already?
I shut my book.
My tea is cold.
Grandpa's never late.
Maybe he said we'd meet at the house first.
I stand and bump the table.
My tea splashes onto the saucer.
I grab my stuff
and hurry out the door.
Something's wrong.

He's sitting on the porch swing.
"Oh." I catch my breath. "There you are, Grandpa.
Shew. Sorry I'm late.
I thought we were meeting at the coffee shop."
I sit down next to him.
"Should I go heat up some water?

Grandpa?"
Drool spills out his mouth,
and he slumps forward.
I catch him. "Grandpa!"

What is wrong?
I jump up
and lay him on his side
on the teetery swing.
"Grandpa! Grandpa!"
I run into the house,
trip over Mija,
and grab the phone.
9-1-1.
"Something's wrong with my grandfather!"

"Please remain on the line."
"I hear the sirens!"
"Do you see the ambulance?"
"Yes, they're here, they're here!"
I slam down the phone.

Two paramedics
rush up the walkway.
"Here! Here's my grandpa.
He won't answer me or anything!"

"Oxygen. And IV."
They are going so fast.
I reach over the swing and hold his hand.
"Please step away," one man tells me.
I jerk my hand back.

"His name?"
"Lawrence Leary," I answer.
"Lawrence, can you hear me?"
Grandpa doesn't wake up.

"Was he speaking when you found him?"
"No, no. He was sitting there.
And then he drooled."

Wires.
Tubes.
Gurney.
Didn't this all just happen to me?

"And your name?"
"Clare. Clare Moller."
"Clare, you've done a good job. Are you here alone?"
"Yes. But I can call my parents.
Grandpa is my mom's dad."

They do more stuff to him.
I pick up Mija and squeeze her tight.

"We will be taking your grandfather
to Valley Hospital."
They wheel Grandpa out to the ambulance.

"Wait!" I set the cat down and run after them.
The gurney slides into the ambulance.
They shut the back doors.
"I, I need to go with him."
"Call your parents
and meet him at the hospital.
We need to leave immediately."
The paramedic
gets into the vehicle.
EeeEeeeEeeee.

"Mom! Something's wrong with Grandpa!"
"What do you mean, Clare?
What?"
"The ambulance took him—"
"Where? Where did they take Dad?"
"Valley Hospital. Mom, come get me first.
Mom, come get me!"
"Hold on, Clare. We're on our way."

Dad's car pulls up.
I dive into the backseat.
"Go!" my mom and I yell.

We speed past neighbors
gathered on the sidewalk.
I didn't even notice them earlier.
"Grandpa was sitting there,
not speaking,
and, and he slumped over,
and I caught him."
Dad races through a yellow light.
"And I couldn't call you right away
because the 9-1-1 lady said
I couldn't hang up the phone."
"You did a good job, Clare," says Dad.
"Now take a breath.
It sounds like everything possible
is being done."
Mom reaches back and grips my hand.
I gasp in a breath
and wipe my tears
on my shoulders.

Alone in the waiting room.
Mom and Dad are storming around
looking for Grandpa,
a nurse, or a doctor
to tell them what's going on.
I'm out of the way here.
Next to the kiddie corner
filled with toys.

God,
I've never prayed
really.
But Grandpa has.
Since he can't talk,
I'm trying.
God,
help Grandpa.
I don't even know what's wrong with him.
He slumped over and
then all that other stuff happened.
And now we're here
and don't even know where he's at.
God, please, please
make Grandpa okay.
Amen.

I walk over to the water fountain.
There's the part of the ER
where I was the other day.
All the curtained-off sections.
What happened
to those poor people
who were here the same time as me?
That little boy with his poked eye,
that man with his back pain?

A boy with his arm in a cast
is wheeled out of the spot I was in.
I take a long drink from the fountain.

I bet the others are all gone.
Back to their lives
that are different now
because they lost control.
Dad's right.
We don't have much control
over anything at all.
Sometimes we just get hurt,
or grow too tall,
or slump over on a porch swing.

The water sloshes around in my stomach.
The fish nip at each other
in the round bubble tank.
The cartoon characters on TV
chase each other.
I clench my hands.
This waiting room is worse
than the ER.
Here you don't know
anything.

It's weird not to call Rosella.
Normally, when something crazy
like this happens,
I'd find a phone
and call her cell.
She's known Grandpa for ages.
I'm sure she cares about him.
It's me she wouldn't want to talk to.
Man, stuff is different now.
And it hurts.

Dad and Mom sit down next to me.
She takes my hand.
"Clare, Grandpa has had a stroke."
"Stroke?"
"A blood vessel burst and the clot
moved to his brain."
"Brain?"
She squeezes my hand.
Dad leans closer. "It looks like
some damage has been done.
But we don't know how much yet."
"His brain?"
Mom sniffles. "We'll get through this."
"Together," says Dad.

"Yes," the doctor says as he turns to Dad,

"there has been some damage.
Preliminary tests are not specific.
But there has been brain damage."
Dad looks down at his shoes.
Mom covers her face.
"So we'll be keeping him in ICU
for observation.
He is stable at this point."
I get up and grab Dad's hand.
"Can we see him?"
"Our policy is only family.
Two visitors at a time."
"Fine," says Dad. "Clare,
wait here,
and we'll be back in a moment."
Mom and Dad follow the doctor
down the hallway.
Hey, I'm family too!
I'm the one that's been living with him!
Me!

I hate the clock.
I hate the TV.
I hate the stupid fish.
It's my grandpa down there.
I
should get to see him.

Ten minutes later
I walk down the hallway
with my head up.
I pass one nurses' station.
No one says anything.
The sign points to the ICU.
I push through another set of doors.
"Can I help you?" a woman asks.
"No."
I walk with purpose
by the hanging curtains
separating beds.
Another nurse steps in front of me.
"I'm sorry. You need to tell me
who you are looking for."
"My grandfather, Lawrence Leary."
She checks her clipboard.
"He's around the corner."
"Thank you." I go to where she pointed.
Mom and Dad are down at the next station.
I peek around the curtain.
"Grandpa!"
I hurry to the bed.
There're machines
everywhere,
and each has a bunch of wires
hooked to him with sticky circles.
Beep. Beep. Beep fills the space.
A little oxygen thing

is stuck in his nose.
"Grandpa?"
He doesn't move or open his eyes.
He is small in the big white bed
and looks weird without his glasses.
I slip my hand around a few wires
and rub his shoulder.
I bend over and kiss his cheek.
Besides the rubbing alcohol
and other mediciney stuff,
I smell his lilac aftershave.
He's still my grandpa.

"Clare!" says Mom.
I jump.
She, Dad, and a nurse
push into the space.
"It was taking too long.
I was waiting and waiting."
"That's okay." Dad puts his arm
around me.
"One of you will need to leave," the nurse says.
She turns away and checks a machine.
"Right," says Dad.
"How about Clare and I go home
and you stay here, Martha."
"Yes. That sounds good."
"But I want to stay," I whine.

"No, we can take care of a few things
while all the testing is being done.
Your mother will call us if there's a change."
"Sure." Mom moves out of the nurse's way
and gives me a hug.
I've never heard her so quiet.
"I, I'll make a dinner for us," I say.
"That would be great, Clare."
She hugs me again
and gives Dad a kiss.
"Bye, Grandpa," I whisper
and follow Dad out.

It's dark.
Dad drives the speed limit.
"I don't know anything about strokes, Dad."
"I think we'll be learning more
than we ever wanted to."
"What's the best it could be
and what's the worst?"
"Don't think about the worst, Clare."
"Come on, Dad."
He rubs the back of his neck.
"Well, the doctor said the best would be
he'd slowly return to normal."
"Yeah, and—"
"The worst would be speech impairment,
inability to walk."

Why did I ask?

I pull out Dad's microwave dinner.
His spaghetti looks a little dry and skinny.
I put a slice of American cheese on top.
That's better.
I load my macaroni and cheese.
It twirls in circles and bubbles.
I bet a taste of this
would cheer Grandpa up.
It's his favorite too.

Nothing new from Mom.
"Go ahead to bed," says Dad.
I get out of Grandpa's chair.
Mija leaps onto it
and curls up.
Does she know?
I hug Dad
and drag my feet to my room.
The book and magazine I bought earlier
are on my nightstand.
Dad must have put them there.
I don't even remember
getting them into the house.
I drag my finger
across the magazine.

I'm worried about not learning to dance,
and Grandpa may never walk again?

All my piled up tears
come out through the night.
This is so horrible
for Grandpa.
It could mean
no walking.
That would mean
no hiking.
No skiing.
Ever again.
No talking!
What then
for him?

I sit on the edge of the couch
and grip my tea cup.
Mom comes in from the kitchen.
"Mom?"
"Yes, sweetheart." Dad rubs his morning whiskers.
"Fill us in."
"Well." She pushes Mija off
and sits down in Grandpa's chair.
The cat hisses and disappears down the hall.
"I took a cab

like we decided, Dwight,
at around five this morning.
I'm completely exhausted,
so if I don't make sense
let me know.
Dad's paralyzed
down his right side.
Most likely permanently."
Mom dabs her eyes.
"And his speech is impaired
because of the damage to the left side of his brain.
He probably won't ever be able
to communicate again verbally."
Dad reaches over and holds her hand.
Mom takes a breath. "The good news is that
he's fully conscious this morning
and seemed to recognize me.
Half his face smiled."
She starts bawling.
Dad rubs her back.
I have to get out of here.

The porch is steaming
from the early morning rain.
The sun bakes the wood,
and the water mists up.
This can't be true, Grandpa.
I flop into the swing.

The mist splits and twists
around me as I rock.
All the sunflowers are facing the sun.
The whole garden is shining.
How can Grandpa be paralyzed,
not be able to talk,
how can he not be here to see
his beautiful garden
this morning?

I wander back inside.
Mom isn't crying anymore.
She's at the dining table
crunched up over some paper.
Dad is reading over her shoulder. "Yes.
That too."
Mom clenches the pencil and snaps it.
"All these changes," she groans.
"It's going to be okay, sweetheart."
Dad massages her shoulders.
"Mom," I say.
They both turn to me.
"What, besides Grandpa,
is changing?"
Mom pats the chair next to her.
"Sit down, Clare.
We need to discuss
everything."

I sit.
"Clare," says Dad,
"we need to make some fast changes."
"Like?"
"Your grandpa
is going to need constant care.
At least for a while."
Mom lines up the pencil pieces
and covers the break
with her shaking thumb and finger.
"I should be focusing on Dad,
but my mind is racing about us."
Dad sits down next to her.
"It's okay.
We're all affected.
We have to look
at our angle as well."

Mom rubs her temple.
"You're right, Dwight.
So.
What I see
is the three of us
move here."
"Whoa. Couldn't Grandpa move in with us
or something?" I ask.
"There isn't enough apartment space, Clare.
Besides, you were looking
into living here before."

"That was *before*," I whisper.
"What?" Dad asks.
"Nothing."

"We'll hire a caregiver
for during the day," says Mom,
"and finally,
the move will mean
responsibility for this house,
which isn't that much different from home,
but there's also the garden."
"I can do that," I say. "The garden, I mean.
Really. I've been helping Grandpa
in the yard since I came."
"That's the spirit, Clare," says Dad.
He takes Mom's hand.
She rests her head against him.
"Our lease is almost up at the apartment."
"Hmm," Dad agrees
and ruffles through the pile of papers.
"It's a good thing
your father gave you power of attorney
a few years back.
It's going to make everything a lot easier."
"Right." Mom's sigh ruffles her bangs.
"Oh, and Clare."
She turns to me.
"It will mean
a change of schools."

"That's not a big deal.
It's not like I had
a ton of friends or anything."
"Well, you'll get to be with Rosella at least."
"Yeah."

So what?

I shut my door behind me.
I've always wanted to live in a house.
And I love Grandpa's.
We've lived in so many different apartments
my whole life
since Mom likes to move.
Starting fresh in new buildings,
over and over.
So now
we are right back where she started.
Her home.
Grandpa's.
Ours.
This really is
my room now.
Not a place to sleep for the summer.
Not a place
in case I made the company.
My room.

I make my bed.
And stuff dirty clothes into the hamper.
I tug out my ballet bag.
The toe shoes are tangled.
I wrap each one carefully.
My skirt is a wadded ball.
I smooth it out and hang it
in the back of the closet.
The whole ballet bag fits perfectly
on the top shelf of my closet.
I shut the door.
We are all starting a new life.
I'm ready to go see Grandpa.

It's nice to pass that emergency sign
and park in the visitors' lot.
An ambulance zooms by.
Somebody else's life is changing.
Maybe ending.

Mom stops me outside the door.
"Even though he isn't in ICU,
I don't want you to be shocked
by his appearance."
"Okay."
"What I mean is that
he looks pretty normal,

but he isn't going to be able to respond to you."
"Okay."
"So act normal."
"Come on, you two." Dad steers both of us
through the door.

"Dad!" Mom bubbles
and gives Grandpa a huge hug.
I hang out at the end of the bed.
Can't even see him yet.
"You are looking
so much better today, Lawrence,"
says Dad in a louder voice than usual.
They both take a seat
on either side of the bed.
"Grandpa?" I say, all trembly.
At least he has his glasses on,
and most of the tubes and wires are gone.
His eyes focus on me,
and half his face smiles.
The other half
looks dead.

"Give Grandpa a kiss, Clare." Mom leans away
so I can reach him.
I kiss
the side that works.
Warm and soft.
He reaches up

and takes my hand.
"Watch his IV," says Mom.
"Martha, Clare knows to be careful."
Dad gives me a wink.
"Yep. I had one of these
a few days ago.
Right, Grandpa?"
"Auuuughh," he says
and drools.
I gasp and look away.
I thought that was only part of the stroke.
He's going to keep drooling?
A tear leaks out of my eye.
"Clare.
It's important
that we keep control,"
Mom says sternly.
But Grandpa rubs my hand.
I look at him again.
Mom finishes wiping his mouth,
but he has a tear now too.

"Would you stay here, Clare,
while we check in
with the doctor?"
"Sure, Dad."
I sit down next to the bed.
For the first time ever,
I'm nervous to be alone

with Grandpa.

"So, this
is a nice room."
He grunts.
"At least no one is in the bed next to you.
You get some privacy."
"Hellooooo!" A nurse busts into the room.
"And how are we, Mr. Leary?"
Oh, great.
We again.
Somebody's mother, I'm sure.
Grandpa smiles
half of his half-smile.

"You can wait
on the other side of the curtain," she says to me.
"Okay."
I stand by the window
as she flings the curtain around the track.
I take a peek over my shoulder.
There's an open space I can see through.
She takes his blood pressure,
his temperature,
checks under his gown.
Why does she have to do that?
I look away fast.
Oh, I bet he's got a catheter!
That's got to be

what that tube was
coming out from down there.
The one draining into the bag
hanging over the bedside.
It was yellow liquid all right.
Yep, pee.
Poor Grandpa!
I bet he's grossing himself out!

"Your bag looks fine, Mr. Leary," she says,
"I'll be back in an hour.
Buzz me if you need anything."
She tugs down Grandpa's gown,
snaps up the sheet,
and slides the curtain aside.
"All done!" She bustles out the door.
"Well, it's sort of private," I say under my breath.

Mom scoops some pudding
into Grandpa's mouth.
Most comes out.
"That's all right, Dad.
It will take some time
to relearn a few things."
She scrapes it off his chin
and smooshes it back in his mouth.
I'm totally sickened,
but I don't want anyone

to know.
I watch,
but
my stomach's squeezy.

"You'll be going home with us soon."
Dad grips Grandpa's foot
through the sheet.
"And we'll be back tomorrow for a visit,"
says Mom.
"Bye," I say.
Grandpa reaches his arm up.
But he's not waving good-bye.
He's asking us to come back.
"Soon, Grandpa.
Soon."
I choke a sob.

"He needs physical therapy
and assisted living."
Mom's voice is squeaking.
"I don't know how we are going
to handle this, Dwight.
The bills will be enormous."
"Take a deep breath, Martha.
Let's get you to the house
so you can sleep.

Everything will seem better then."
She sniffles.
"I'll check in at the bookstore.
Clare can straighten up
while you rest.
Let's take this day by day.
Okay?"
She stares straight ahead.

What will the days
be like?

Now I know.
We have breakfast together.
Dad goes to work.
Mom and I go to the hospital.
I read to Grandpa and work the crossword
so he can see it.
Mom scoops in his lunch.
Then she goes with him to physical therapy
to learn what exercises
she'll do with him at home.
That's when I smooth out his bed
and water the flowers
his church friends have sent.
Throw out the dying ones.
Then I flip on the TV and chill for a while.

We get Grandpa back into his bed
and say good-bye.
That's the worst part.
Then we head to the house.
I clean up and do laundry.
Mom works over the bills and insurance.
I garden.
Which is the only time I even think about ballet,
and how different my life is
without one plié.
Mom and I cook dinner.
Dad gets home.
We eat,
read, watch TV,
then get to bed early
to start again.
Over and over.
Day by day.

I dig out all the daylilies
along the front of the house.
The bulbs are clumped tight.
I pull and cut them apart carefully
and lay them in the wheelbarrow.
The pulpy white roots dangle exposed.

I pick the grit out from under my nails

as the work truck pulls into the driveway.
Two construction workers
bang an ugly ramp together
in a few hours.
It runs long to get a gentle slope
up to the big front porch.
They had to take out the side railing
for the landing.

Mom writes a check and they pull away.
I get down in the dirt
and replant the flowers
next to the ramp.
I'm trying to break up that long line.
Everything else in Grandpa's garden
is planted to make gentle curves.
Even the house has the sloped Tudor roof.
The daylilies don't help much.
The ramp is one long eyesore.

The moving company
cleared everything
out of our apartment
and dumped it here
in one day.
I didn't even get a chance
to say good-bye to my room.

Not that it was all that special,
but still.
It's something I always do
before we move.
How do I know
they got
all my stuff?

I step around the boxes
stacked in the living room.
At least the big furniture is still out in the garage.
How will we fit
all our stuff in
with Grandpa's?
Somebody is going to have to
get rid of things.
Especially with our giant book collection.
I slide a couple boxes to the wall
to make a path.
Mija sharpens her claws on a cardboard tower.
At least someone
likes this mess.

"Donation
or storage," says Dad.
"Or garage sale," Mom adds.

Dad glances at me. "What do you think?"
I look over Mom's itemized list
of our stuff and Grandpa's.
There are a lot of twos
running down the quantity column.
"I think we should save
as many of Grandpa's things
as we can."
"Me too," says Dad.
"It will make Lawrence feel like it's his home
even though we've moved in."
"I'd like to keep
my kitchenware, though," says Mom.
"He won't notice that," I say. "But
let's keep his couch and definitely his chair."
"Absolutely," Mom says.
"Then we can donate or have a sale
to get rid of what we don't want."
"That sounds like a plan," says Dad.
He puts his arm around us both.
It's good to have a plan
we all agree to.
Too bad Grandpa doesn't get a vote.

I drop into bed,
surrounded by boxes.
At least we got the kitchen unpacked.
I can work in here

tomorrow.
Even if everything is out of sight
it's nice to have my stuff close by.
Grandpa's got to be anxious to come home soon
and be near his own stuff.

Grandpa can
halfway smile,
hold and squeeze my hand,
listen,
make grunting sounds,
chuckle,
drool,
dribble food,
and get from the wheelchair
to the toilet
and then back to the chair
if someone helps.
(Not me.)
But that means no catheter!
Which is great.
Um . . .

That's
about
it.

We go for a walk.
Not on a trail around a lake
or up a mountain path.
Grandpa and I
walk
around and around
the twelfth floor
of the hospital
in the brand-new wheelchair
Dad got him.
I walk and push,
and he
rides.
"Again, Grandpa?"
He grunts and points.
We go again.

I dump year-old candy into the trash.
The movers definitely brought everything
from my old room.
Oh, here are all my posters.
I open the tube and tug them out.
Dancers spread across my bed.
A hotness sears my stomach.
Maybe I can store these or something.
No way can they go up on my walls.
And I can't dump them.
It'd be like tossing out a part of me.

Only because I've had them forever.

I stack the curling posters.
I might as well add Baryshnikov to them.
That corner's still peeling up.
I tug the poster off the wall
and add it to the pile.
The roll slides easily back into the tube.
I toss the whole thing into a storage box.

The last box is empty.
Finally.
I flop onto my bed.
It looks different
from my room at home.
I like this old bed Grandpa had in here.
It's more comfy than mine,
which is why I told Dad I wanted it instead.
And the antique dresser.
Everything's less crowded,
even with the rest of my books from home.
So much stuff ended up in storage.
All the ballet trinkets and knickknacks.
My bulletin board is empty.
What will I put up there now?
No ticket stubs from performances.
No photos of famous dancers.
It's absolutely blank.

Kinda scary.

Oops. Those sticky blobs where my poster was
are still up there.
I dig my thumbnail under each
and peel them up.
Little oil circles are left behind.
I'll have to get some other poster to cover them.
Some other thing I'm into.
What was Dia going to try?
Lacrosse?
No way does that interest me.
Will anything ever?

"What is it, Grandpa?"
He points and grunts.
"Candy?"
He shakes his head and points.
"The flowers?"
No.
I get up and go over to the corner
he's looking at.
"What? The book? You want me to read
out loud?"
No.
"Ugh. This is so
frustrating."
He keeps pointing.

"The clock?"
No.
"I wish you could tell me,
could say it."
I scoot the flowers around
and look for something
he sees that I don't.
"If you could talk, Grandpa,
I'd listen to every one of your stories,
even the super-duper long ones
I've heard a zillion times."
He smiles.
"The crossword?"
No.
"Oh, look at this cute teddy bear."
He nods.
"You want the bear?"
No.
He points at me.
"Thanks, Grandpa."

"We believe your father will be ready
to be released next week."
The doctor snaps the cover of the file
closed.
Mom jumps.
"Physical therapy will need to be continued,
but he is completely stable,

and there is no reason
he can't go home."
"Excellent!" I say, and relevé
up on my toes.
Yikes. Mom didn't see,
she's still talking to the doctor.
But
Grandpa did.
And he's smiling
at my feet.

Dad divvies up the teriyaki.
"Hey, a little more over here."
I shove my plate closer.
"It's nice to see you eat, Clare."
He loads on more meat.
"Mm. Thanks for picking this up, Dwight."
Mom wipes sauce off her lips.
"Well, we needed it.
After the work we did this week,
combining two households,
we all deserved a treat." Dad takes a big bite.
"This is delicious," he says.
I swallow. "Yeah,
it's Grandpa's favorite teriyaki takeout."
"Was this the restaurant on the corner of Main,"
asks Mom,

"or the one by the high school,
or the one by the grocery?"
"The one by the German bakery," Dad and I say.
Mom grins. "Western Washington is being
taken over
by coffee stands and teriyaki takeouts."
"Perfect to me." I crunch into an egg roll.
"Okay, we'll do this when Dad's home.
With the hope that he'll work up to
eating solids again."
"Right." I scoop some rice onto my plate.
"He's the one
who really needs a treat.
And this one
he's sure to love."

Mom takes a sip of coffee
and pushes her empty plate away.
"It is bizarre
living in my childhood room
with my husband," says Mom.
Dad chuckles.
"Don't you think it's weird for me?"
She smiles. "Absolutely. It's one thing to visit
or sleep over,
but another to actually move back in."
"That's why I picked the guest room

when I first came," I say.
"I thought it was spooky
Grandma never redecorated
after you left, Mom."
"She liked everything the same.
No changes,
anyway, anyhow." She pauses.
"Seeing Dad like he is
would have torn her up.
I'm kind of glad she isn't here now."
"Probably best." Dad licks his fork clean.
"But think about it."
"What?" Mom asks.
"She'd really like the fact that
you're finally going to keep your room clean."
We all laugh.
"So *The Muppet Movie* poster
is coming down?" I ask.
"Hey, I like Kermit," Dad cuts in.
"Okay, you two." Mom stands
and clears the table.
"Maybe Kermit can stay up,
but the Bee Gees have to come down."
"Definitely," I say with a giggle.

Getting piles of forms signed.
Getting lectures from nurses
on life at home after a stroke.

Getting booklets, instructions,
and pamphlets.
Getting all Grandpa's stuff together.
Mom getting him dressed.
Dad getting the van.
Let's get Grandpa out of here!

I slide the van door open.
Dad hits the controls and lowers the chairlift.
The attendant rolls Grandpa onto the metal
and locks his wheelchair in place. "There you go."
Grandpa's chair rises in the air.
He clenches the armrest.
"It's okay, Grandpa," I call.
I hurry around and jump in on the other side.
His chair slides in next to my seat.
"See?" I reach over and hold his hand.
"Let's blow this place."
He grunts.
Mom gets in the front.
Dad starts the engine.
"Good-bye, hospital!" I shout.
Grandpa raises a celebration fist.

The long freight train rumbles past.
Dad inches up to the blinking crossing arm.
"How do you like your new wheels, Lawrence?"

"Grgh," says Grandpa.
Dad turns around in his seat. "We got a good deal
trading in your car.
This baby is smooth."
"Hey, Smooth. The train's gone," says Mom.
Dad turns back and guns it over the tracks.
I wink at Grandpa. "Smooth."

He's sitting in his wheelchair on the porch
and crying.
Oh, what am I supposed to do?
Mom and Dad are inside
working on paperwork or something.
"Here, Grandpa." He takes the tissue
and swipes at his face.
"Let me." I take it back
and wipe his tears and nose.
It feels huge compared to mine.
Weird.
"Come on, Grandpa.
You're home.
Everything is going to be okay.
It's just that things are different."
He looks up at me.
"You get your same room at least.
And we get to live with you all the time.
It's only a little more crowded
than you are used to."

He grunts.
"Did you see I moved the daylilies?"
He almost smiles.
"I didn't want to lose them
when the ramp was built.
So I dug the bulbs up and replanted
them. It looks like they are taking
to the new spot.
That's not so easy sometimes."

"Mija's missed you
so much."
I pick her up.
Grandpa smiles.
"She pretty much
stayed in your chair
the whole time
you were in the hospital."
I set her down
in Grandpa's lap.
He curls his good arm
around her.
The cat licks
his paralyzed hand.

Mom joins us on the porch.
"Be right back," Dad calls from his car.
"Where's he going, Mom?"

"Running to the store for a few things.
She wheels Grandpa into the house.
The extra little slope
the ramp guys made
makes it easy for the chair to glide into the house.

Mom pushes Grandpa to the window
and puts his brake on.
"Your friends
are coming over to hold your prayer group here."
Grandpa smiles and smooths his shirt.
"Bruce—
the one I met at the hospital—
he said they'd be willing to meet here regularly."
"Is that okay, Grandpa?" I ask.
He nods.
"I'll put some water on for tea," says Mom.
"They should be here within a half hour."
I follow Mom to the kitchen.

"Does his group need to come now?"
"We need to create
some normalcy for him, Clare.
Bruce told me
Dad's prayer group meets
the first Monday of the month.
Seeing his friends will help.
It's only for an hour."
"I don't know, Mom.

It seems too fast.
I mean, we just got him home
a couple hours ago.
He must be tired.
What's it going to feel like
to be stared at by all of them
at once?
He's so different now,
and not like them—"
"Clare." Mom rubs my shoulder.
"It's okay. These are his friends."
I take a big breath. "Right."

As soon as Dad got back from the store,
he and Mom set out snacks.
Then they both disappeared.
Figures.
I stare at this woman
with super-stiff platinum hair,
and oversized white, white teeth
that click.
She's gobbling me up.
"Oh, yes. You're the dancer.
Your grandfather always speaks of you."
"I'm not really a dancer. I didn't make it into—"
"Now, now.
I've heard far too much about you.
Your grandfather says

you feel the music.
You move from your heart."
"Yeah. Well. Um."
"It's very nice to meet you, Clare.
I need to join the others.
We're starting our meeting.
Did you want to join—
No? Well, that's okay, dear.
I'll look forward to chatting with you
another time."

I slip away to the bathroom
and splash cold water on my face.
My intestines are braided in knots.
I swallow hard to keep my stomach down.
Why did Grandpa ever say all that stuff?

No way I'm a dancer.
What do I do every day?
Stuff around the house.
Stuff for Grandpa.
I'm a
maid-gardener-nurse.

What's Rosella doing every day?
Dancing in City Ballet.
Taking a moment
to puke
after class.

Taking a break
in the coffee shop
to laugh at people
who didn't make it.
Bottom line: dancing.

She's a dancer.

What about Elton?
Dancing in the company.
He does have to work in the bookstore.
But big deal.
That's not like babysitting your Grandpa.
Elton probably doesn't even think
of me anymore.
Why would he?
He's busy being a dancer.

Okay.
Get a grip.
It's one old lady.
Who cares what she thinks?

No big deal.
I'm moving on
from ballet,
from my old apartment,
from my old school,
from so-called friends.

I'm moving on.
I just can't think of
where to go.

I peek around the corner.
What's a prayer meeting like anyway?
Ballet lady has her back to me.
That's good.
Everyone's so smiley
and chatty.
Most of them are pretty old
like Grandpa.
Whoa.
The one lady with cat eyeglasses
is dabbing Grandpa's handkerchief
to his mouth.
That's pretty nice.
Huh.
They seem to really like him.
Even though he's so different now.

That one guy, Bruce,
is reading from a Bible.

Now they are talking about
what to pray for.
One man

says to pray for Grandpa.
That's nice.

Now they are praying.
And praying.
And praying.

Done finally.

What's with the harmonica?
Oh. Hymns.
Huh. They don't sound half bad
if you like that kind of music.
Grandpa sure seems to like it,
the way he's rocking and smiling.

Everyone's lining up
to shake his left hand
or give him a hug.
So that's a prayer meeting.
It doesn't seem
all that strange.

"What an interesting painting."
Bruce clips his pen
into his shirt pocket.
He peers more closely

at the picture by the door.
"Do you know the story behind it, Clare?"
"Sure.
Grandpa's told me tons
of times. It's the land his grandfather owned
before he came to America.
It's back in Switzerland."
"How nice. It's delightful.
Well, I'd best be off."

I shut the door behind him.
I'm glad I remembered the story
about the painting.
Sure, Mom might have known about it too,
but there's probably stuff she doesn't know.
Things Grandpa only told me.
I turn around and bump into his wheelchair.
He reaches up
for my hand.
I remembered about the painting.
But what about other stories
he never got to tell?
Those I'll never get to hear.

Dad suddenly appears
and pushes Grandpa to the window.
"You can wave
as your friends leave, Lawrence," he says.

"Clare, come help
with dinner," Mom calls from the kitchen.

"So, what did you think of that?" she asks.
"Seriously."
"It seemed nice enough, I guess."
She passes me lettuce and tomatoes.
"Would you work on the salad?
Fix a big one.
I'm really hungry."
"Sure." I get out a paring knife.

"Well, I hope that's sufficient for him," she says.
"That's all I can say, Clare. Really."
"What do you mean?"
She pounds the cube steak with a mallet.
"I hope hosting
the prayer meeting once a month
is enough for Dad.
We don't want to have to take him
to church every week."

The knife breaks through the thin tomato skin.
Seeds spill out along the blade.
"But that's really important to Grandpa."
"I know it is." She slams the steak.
"But we all need to give in a little, Clare.
You, your father, and I
don't need to join the church.

I had enough in my childhood."
"Yeah. But he looked so happy.
Mom, I could push him there.
I wouldn't mind.
It's only a couple blocks."

Bam. Bam.

"It's not convenient for us.
We need some normalcy too."
Convenient for *us*? What about Grandpa?
He's already giving up
his book club and Bible study.
I mince the tomato into tiny bits.

Mom lies down on the couch.
"Moving Dad around is exhausting."
"Yeah, but he's
even more tired
with the excitement of coming home
and the prayer meeting."
"You're right, Clare."

I flop on the floor
and stretch into a split.
Oh, that feels great.
My muscles are already tight
from not taking class.

Mom looks over
and raises an eyebrow.
"That's strange to see."
What am I doing?
I pull my legs in
and cross them.
"What?"
"You doing ballet."
"I wasn't. I just wasn't thinking
for a minute."
I'm
an idiot.

"I know things have been
completely hectic," says Mom.
Here we go.
"But have you given any thought
to yourself, honey?"
"Not really. We've been too busy."
"I can give you that.
But
are you sleeping well,
having bad dreams,
missing classes—"
"I'm fine, Mom."
"Are you—"
"Fine."
"Okay. I only want you to know

I'm here for you."

There's no doubt about that.
Sometimes I don't want to talk about
every little thing.
Even if it was okay
talking to her about the audition.
Sometimes
it's nice to keep a bit to yourself.
Stuff maybe you haven't even figured out yet.
Be your own person that way.
I can't explain that
to her.

She's already talking again.
"It was such a big dream,
and now with Dad's stroke,
I don't want to neglect you, sweetheart."
"I'm fine."
She humphs.
"Okay, Clare.
If you say so.
I may not be fine.
Not that anyone's asked.
I may be worn down
to a bloody nub,
but I'm glad
you
are fine."

She crosses her arms.
Someone's cranky tonight. . . .

"That shower chair worked well.
I got him washed,
dressed, and into bed." Dad
collapses at the end of the couch.
Mom plops her feet onto his lap.
"Thanks, Dwight.
Being a man,
Dad's got to be more comfortable
with you showering him than me."
"I hope it saves some of his dignity."
"Yes." Mom covers her eyes
with her arm. "I can't get over
how much work this is.
We are wiped out after one day.
But everything will be easier
when we get assistance.
We should have a worker
by midweek, right?"
"Right."
Mom sighs. "If the daily routine is this hard,
imagine what an undertaking it will be
to get him to physical therapy next week.
We definitely need help."
"Will the worker be a man, Dad?"
"No, I think the service is sending a woman."

"That's not going to feel so great
to Grandpa."
"Well," says Mom, "we'll try to make Dad
feel comfortable when we can.
Like your dad showering him.
But we need help, Clare.
Anything, from anyone,
at this point
will be appreciated."
"Okay already," I say.
Dad pokes my leg
and massages Mom's foot.
"Sounds like we could all use
some extra sleep," he says.
"Yeah," I mutter. "It's crab city around here."
Mom gives me a look.
I get up
and hug the bloody nub anyway, then Dad.

Poor Grandpa.
What man
would want some strange woman
to help him in the bathroom
and stuff?
Who would want anyone to help them
in the bathroom and stuff?

I step into the tub.

Huh. My feet don't burn now.
I sit down and prop them up on the wall.
Wow. All the blisters are healing over.
My feet still look gross,
but mostly they're bumpy, red, and callused.
That's amazing.
I dunk them back underwater.
Things heal fast.
Well,
some things.
Other things never get better.
Grandpa's paralyzed side of his body
still grosses me out.
It's like he's not even in that dead part.
I don't like to touch the pasty skin.
What's it feel like to him?
What's it feel like
not to be able to feel?
I slide my head underwater.
I can't imagine.

Grandpa squints in the morning sun.
Mom tucks a blanket on his lap
and turns to me.
"I'll register you at the school,
pick up Dad's medications,
and be back before you know it."
Mom drops her keys on the sidewalk.

I bend down and hand them to her.
"Are you sure,
absolutely sure
you'll be fine?" she asks.
"Yeah, Mom. Trust me.
I can be responsible."
Grandpa grunts and waves to her.
"See? He agrees." I urge her toward
the car. "Dad took him to the bathroom
before he left. You'll be back
before he needs to go again.
I'm going to wheel him around the block.
Maybe stop for tea at the coffee shop."
"That sounds like too much, Clare."
"Mom, I pushed him around the hospital
a lot. It won't be any different."
"All right. But take some cash."
She presses money into my hand.
"Go, Mom."
"Okay, okay."
Finally
she gets in the car
and drives away.
She leaves me alone
with Grandpa.

I lean into the chair.
Grandpa's wheels bump over the roots

breaking through the sidewalk.
He grips the chair arm
with his good hand.
"It's okay, Grandpa. I've got you."
This is way harder
than going over smooth hospital floors.
I roll him to the corner and wait for the light.
The cars slow and stop.
"Here we go."
It's this stupid short light.
We have to hurry or we are going to be stuck
in the middle.
I push him across the street,
and he grunts and waves his arm.
"What? I can't stop in the street
and figure out what you're saying, Grandpa."
"Gruggrrr."
I lean into the chair and push him up the incline
onto the opposite sidewalk.
"What is it, Grandpa?"
He points to the conservatory,
points at me,
and bangs the armrest.
The conservatory.
"Yeah, I see it. So?"
He points at me again,
then at the building.
"Come on, Grandpa.
Let's go."

He bangs the armrest once more,
but stops grunting.
He never would have done all that
before the stroke.
Even his personality is different.
And right now,
I don't like it.

There's a break in the traffic,
and music streams out the barre room window
above us.
Grandpa sways his head.
I focus on pushing him around the people
walking so easily on the sidewalk.
It's hard to get from one place to another
without running into or over someone.
I bump into a businessman.
He gives me an angry look.
"Sorry," I mumble.
He hurries off.
Why does everything
have to be so hard?

The bookstore
is straight across the street.
I wheel Grandpa as fast as I can.
Don't look.
Don't look.

I do.
Elton isn't at the register.
It's some lady with a ponytail.
I shouldn't have looked,
and then I could have kept pretending
he was there.
Close by.

"Clare!"
Oh, great.
It's Devin.
"Hi, Clare.
How are you doing?
I'm so sorry you didn't make it.
And who is this?
Your grandpa?
Hello!
You really would have made it, Clare,
if you weren't tall.
You know that, don't you?
Because you are *such* a good dancer.
I mean it.
Well, it's great to see you.
And nice to meet you.
I have to hurry.
Rehearsal's in half an hour.
I'll tell the other girls
how great you look.

You really do.
Keep in touch.
Bye."
She skitters away.
Grandpa looks up at me,
chuckling.
Devin chatters more than Mom!
Who knew?
People are so different
outside of class.
Well,
at least I didn't have to think
of one thing
to say.

I push Grandpa to the park
and stop on the pavement
near the biggest maple tree.
This is the one
with the sculpture
hanging in it.
The plaque says it's by Anthony Howe.
Grandpa and I
watch the slowly twirling
circles, cups, and stainless steel arms
moving in different directions
above our heads.

It shines and spins in silence.
A perfect spiral dance
in the breeze.

I set the brake on Grandpa's chair
and sit down on the warm asphalt.
"We made it."
He grunts.
I lean against his wheel.
Some little kids
are playing hide-and-seek.
I recognize the mayor,
who's served so many terms,
pushing her grandson on the swing.
She's someone as identifiable to this town
as the judge
and the daffodils.
Small towns can be cool.
Even this one,
with the conservatory
hovering like a ghost on Main Street.
It will be fun living where Mom grew up.
The Daffodil Parade in spring,
outdoor concerts later in summer.
I've heard the high school is pretty tight.
In a couple years
I'll be a Spartan like Mom was.
A new life and new friends.

Grandpa brushes my head.
I look up.
He's smiling down at me.
In one half of his face
I see
Grandpa
and the spinning sculpture
glinting above him.

I close my eyes
and listen.
Children laughing.
"Joey," a mom calls.

The chair squeaks
as Grandpa shifts.

Poplar leaves
shshsh in the light wind.

"Oooh. Yuck.
Drooly drool!"
A kid's pointing
at my grandfather.
"Oooooh," he squeals, and runs
to his friends.
I jump up

and wipe Grandpa's mouth
with his handkerchief.
"I'm sorry, Grandpa.
I'm sorry."
He hangs his head.
"Let's get out of here."
I release the brake
and roll him away
from their laughter.

"Do you want to stop for tea?" I ask.
He shakes his head.
"Okay, we'll go home."
We walk and roll
all the way home
in silence.

Grandpa pushes the gate open
with his good arm,
and I push him through.
We both let out a big sigh.
"Home," I say,
park him by the sunflowers,
and set the brake.
"Do you want some tea now?"
He grunts.
"Okay, I'll be right back."

The kettle shrieks.
I pour the boiling water
over the bag,
stir in some honey,
and head back out.

"Grandpa!" I call.
A sun shower mists down on him.
He grins at me.
"It's raining! Come on."
I set his cup down on the stair
and rush over to him.
He bats my arm away from the brake.
"Grandpa, we have to get you onto the porch.
It's raining."
He grunts
and swats my arm.
"What? I don't know what
you're saying."
He stares at me.
I wipe the water off my face.
I try one more time.
He bangs the armrest,
and I start crying the tiniest bit.
Why can't he speak
for once?
Even if it was like before,
and he'd run on and on.
Why can't he speak?

"Ughgh," I groan.

Grandpa grabs my hand
and holds it up to the sky.
I look up.
The droplets land on my eyelashes.
The sun warms my neck.

Grandpa is smiling again.
Rain washes his glasses.
We hold hands
by the sunflowers.

"Clare!" Mom yells.
I drop Grandpa's hand.
She slams the car door.
"What are you thinking?"
"I—"
"Get Dad inside right now.
It's pouring.
He's soaked!"
She thrusts shopping bags into my hands
and shoves by to the back of the wheelchair.
"Never mind. I'll do it. Honestly, Clare!"
Mom releases the brake
and wheels Grandpa up the ramp.
"Everything is wet!
I'll have to get a rag to dry the wheels

before I can even take him inside."
The storm door bangs behind her.
"Urghph." Grandpa turns in the chair
and holds his arm up to me.
He's smiling.
I set down the bags,
hold my arms up
to the sun,
and relevé.
My entire body
stretches
anxiety
out.

"It took me twenty minutes
to change him out of those damp clothes."
Mom fixes Grandpa's
dry shirt collar.
She tucks the fleece blanket
over his lap.
I shrink into the couch
in my robe
and pull Mija onto my lap.
She nips my hand and jumps down.
"I need to be able to trust you, Clare,"
says Mom. "I need you to think
about what you are doing."
"I tried to bring him inside—"

"Tried isn't good enough."
"He was batting my hand away,
and I couldn't even get to the brake."
"Excuses.
You may have lowered his resistance,
and now he could catch a cold.
I can't have you saying you're
responsible and then showing
you aren't."
"Mom," I raise my voice, "I am.
I took him to the park.
We were fine."
I push away the thought
of the little kid making fun.
"He said he wanted to sit in the rain."
"Please, Clare. He *said*?
I don't know what's wrong with you.
Maybe you are overwhelmed
with everything lately."
"What is that supposed to mean?"
"With the failure—the changes we've had—
maybe it's too much."
"I'm fine," I say with my teeth clenched.
Grandpa bangs his armrest.
Mom and I jump.
He points at the couch.
"What is it, Dad?"
He points again.
"Dad, I see Clare on the couch."

He slaps the armrest harder.
I get up and push his chair.
"He wants you to move him
over to the couch."
"Are you sure?" Mom asks.
I don't answer.
Grandpa leans over
and digs behind a pillow.
He pulls out a harmonica.
"Oh, that must have been left behind
from the prayer meeting." Mom reaches for it.
"Come on, Dad.
I'll put it in a safe place."
Grandpa holds it away from her.
"Dad."
"He wants it himself, Mom."
"I can see that."
She struggles to snatch it,
and he pushes her away.
"Fine! I'll call Bruce
and let him know it's here."
Mom storms off to the kitchen.
Grandpa turns the harmonica
over and over.
He brings it up and presses it to his lips.
"Ooooooooohhhh." One long, eerie note
comes out.
"Clare, stop.
Don't play with that.

It's not ours." Mom comes
back into the room
and stares at Grandpa.
He takes another big breath.
Several notes slide out
one right after another.
I take a big breath
each time he does.
Somehow, he cups one hand
over the instrument
and moves it back and forth.
The notes are slurred a little,
but I recognize the song.
It's Mozart.
The music quivers my skin.
He pulls the harmonica
away from his face.
He's weeping.
He's talked
to us.

We both rush over and hug him.
"I'm home," calls Dad.
"I found this cup of tea on the porch.
Hey, what's all this about?"
"Grandpa can play the harmonica!" I shout.
"What?"
"He can. He can!"

"Martha, did you know he could?"
"No." Mom stands and wipes her face.
"I didn't. I've never seen him, ever before."
Dad sets the cup on the side table.
"Show me, Lawrence," he says.
"Wait." I wipe Grandpa's drool
with his handkerchief.
"Okay. Go ahead and show him."
This time Grandpa plays a faster song.
Mom claps,
Dad laughs,
and I do some fancy footwork.
Grandpa is showing
there still is some joy
in his heart,
and we are showing
ours right back.

The moon lights Mom's face.
She nudges the porch swing.
I lean my head back.
"I can't believe Dad played for over an hour."
"Me either."
Mija slinks out of the shadow
and jumps up onto my lap.
She turns around and around
then sits.
A perfect circle of fur.

"And then he played again after dinner," I say.
Mom yawns. "I put the harmonica
right next to his bed
when I tucked him in."
"That's good."
We rock in the dark.
A slow sad song drifts out of the house.
"I better go check on him.
Something could be wrong."
"No." I pull her back down. "Just listen."
Grandpa plays into the night,
and we rock
in rhythm.

She said
failure
when we were fighting.
It had to have been about City Ballet.
I spit into the sink
and rinse my toothbrush.
I know it.
I failed.
But when she says it,
it makes me mad.
I twist the faucet off.
When she says it,
I want to fight back
and show her

she's wrong.
Even though
she's right.

I'm so tight.
My muscles
feel like cement.
I grip the iron footboard
of my bed
and plié.
That's never felt so good.

I peep at the clock.
7:00.
Ugh.
It's so early.
Voices murmur,
bags rustle.
Maybe Mom and Dad need help
with Grandpa.
I stumble out of my room.
"Well, hey there!" A very large woman
smiles at me.
She's like between Mom and Grandpa's age.
"Uh, hi."
"Clare, this is Mabel." Mom
reaches over and straightens

my long T-shirt.
I flinch from her cold fingers.
"It's mighty nice to meet you, Clare."
Mabel straightens her white uniform
over her large lumpy body.
"I'm looking forward to taking
good care of your granddaddy for you."
"Great," I say. "I, um,
forgot you were coming today.
I'll go get dressed."
"And, Mabel, if you'd come with me,"
Mom says, heading to the kitchen.

I slip on my jeans and a clean T-shirt.
Wow. I knew a woman was coming,
but this one is so big.
She fills the whole room.
Will Grandpa like her?
At least she doesn't look like one of those freaks
who hurt old people.
There was that news report
I watched with Dad one time.
Those guys steal and are rough,
and no one ever finds out
because the patients usually can't talk
or don't realize they're being hurt.
I pull my brush
through my hair.

Mabel's deep laugh
rolls to my room.
Grandpa's going to like
this lady.

Dad wheels Grandpa out from his room.
Mom hurries along beside to comb his hair
one last stroke.
"Hey there, Mr. Lawrence. I'm Mabel."
She reaches down
and shakes Grandpa's hand.
She covers his hand with her other
and looks him in the eye.
"Pleased to meet you, sir."
"Grumgrh." Grandpa smiles.
Friends already?

"Mabel, are you sure
you can handle Dad alone
on your first day?
Especially when we have an early start
at the store?" asks Mom.
"Ma'am, we'll be fine.
Clare can help
with any questions. Right?"
"Yeah."
Mabel reaches over

and squeezes me against her.
She's soft and squishy.
"They'll be fine, Martha." Dad
gets his briefcase,
gives me a kiss on the forehead,
and herds Mom out.

"Bye." We wave from the porch.
"What is that beautiful sound?" Mabel asks.
"Oh, it's Grandpa.
We found out yesterday
he can play the harmonica."
Mabel hums the tune
and goes back in the house.

The two
together
sound beautiful.

She fed him breakfast
like it was no big deal,
and it took half as long as when
Mom or Dad do it.
"Race ya!" she called,
and zoomed through Grandpa's room
tidying up everything
before I could get my own done.
Of course, mine was much messier than his

at the start.
Now she's ironing his shirts,
pressing perfect creases down the arms.
I brush out Mija, who stretches and purrs.
"It can get kind of boring
around here sometimes."
"How 'bout a game?" The iron steams up
around Mabel's arm.
"You want to play a game?"
"No. How 'bout a game for you and
your granddaddy?"
"Like what?"
"How 'bout checkers?"
"I think we have a set somewhere.
You want to play checkers, Grandpa?"
He grunts.
"Okay."
Who ever would have thought
of that?

Mabel sets down the phone.
"That wasn't your mother
checking on us again.
It was Bruce. He asked me to tell the family
Mr. Lawrence can go ahead
and keep that harmonica."
"That's nice. Did you hear that, Grandpa?"

He's smiling.
He heard all right.

We face off
at the coffee table.
"Are you sure he can do this, Mabel?"
"Give him a chance," she says.

The pieces shake in Grandpa's hand,
and sometimes he bumps the board.
But he can play.
He wins the first game.
I win the second.
Grandpa bangs his armrest,
but he's grinning.
I scoop up all the black and red circles
and dump them in the box.
"Good game."

Mabel comes into the living room.
"Mr. Lawrence, would you like a cup of coffee?"
He grunts yes.
"I'm going out to garden." I stand.
"Alrighty, then."
Mabel pulls Grandpa back
and whisks him to the kitchen.

She is super strong.
But so big. What's that like?
To have so much more of you
all around your bones.
To shake and jiggle
when you move.
I felt how soft it is
when she hugged me.
Soft and round.
I poke my hip bone
pushing out against my jeans.
It's a hard, sharp edge.
I suck my stomach in
till it caves backward.
I can't imagine
what it's like
to be fat.

The pansies are getting leggy,
spreading out real far.
I pinch off the wilted flowers.
Each plant looks stronger
without the dead stuff hanging on.
Mabel's hums slip out the window to me.
Grandpa joins her with his harmonica.
What is that song?
I pull a ladybug off my sleeve
and set it on a rose leaf.

"A mighty fortress is our God," Mabel
sings loudly.
Oh, yeah. That's a little familiar.
Did they sing it at the prayer meeting?
I stand up. Her deep alto voice
vibrates into my muscles.
Such a powerful song.
I bring my arms up to fifth position
then down again.
Relevé
and take a deep bow
on the last note.
Perfect.

Mabel tosses the salad.
"Nothing like fresh basil leaves
in a salad. Mmhm. That is some garden
you have, Mr. Lawrence."
Grandpa grins.
I pull out a chair and sit down.
Mija circles Mabel's wide ankles.
"And you sure do have
a beautiful kitty," she adds.
Grandpa waves at the cat.
"You have a beautiful voice, Mabel," I say.
"Well, thank you."
"Did you ever sing professionally?"
"Oh, for a bit."

She adds some dressing to the lettuce
and pops a couple olives into her mouth.
"I did sing for a time on stage,
but I didn't enjoy it."
"Why not?"
"Why not. Well." She chomps
a cherry tomato. "I found
when I sang professionally,
it wasn't as fun for me. The nerves,
the practices, the pressure."
"Yeah. I know what you're saying."
"Before I knew it,
all the beauty and fun of singing
were gone."
She tosses the salad.
"I know some people can go out
and sing
and the performing fills them up.
That was never me."
"Huh."
"Yep. So I stopped
and sang again for myself
or sometimes for the church.
All my joy for song came back."
"Because you were doing it for you?"
"Exactly."
I look at Grandpa.
He's beaming.

I wander downtown.
It's nice to be able to go
alone.
Having Mabel to be with Grandpa
is going to be great.
I'll read in the park,
then get a cup of tea.
Everything is so normal,
even when our lives have totally changed.
I walk down the busy sidewalk,
right by the conservatory.
I'm not afraid of it.
"Excuse me," says a woman pushing a double
stroller.
I lean back against the wall
so she can get by.
My fingers brush the smooth brick.
"And one and two," Madame's voice
sifts down from the floor room windows.
My fingernails rake the rough mortar.
"And reach. Hold it. Hold it. Release."
I pull away from the building
and flow with the crowd
down the sidewalk.

On the other side of the street,
Tommy's talking to Elton outside the bookstore.
It's great to see Elton!

Tommy looks pretty cute in street clothes too.
I wonder if he acts any more decent?
Elton sees me and waves.
I wave back.
He gestures for me to come over.
But the crosswalk is way down at the end
of the block,
and traffic is thick.
Now Tommy gives me a little wave too.
I give a good-bye, see-you-around shrug.
Hopefully they buy it.
They don't need to waste their time
talking to me.
I'm sure they are super busy
with rehearsals,
like Devin said.
What do I have
to talk to them about anyway?

Mom and Dad come home.
He starts dinner while she fusses all around
making sure Grandpa is okay.
Mabel gets ready to leave.
"You'll come back, won't you?" I ask.
"Surely, surely."
"Tomorrow?"
"Bright and early."
"Okay."

"So long now."
"Bye," I call,
and watch her drive away
in her long beige car.
She has to
come back.

"Clare, where are my olives?"
I look away from the TV.
"What, Mom?"
"I had a jar of olives in the refrigerator,
and they're gone."
"Oh, I think Mabel nibbled on them today."
I stretch out on the couch.
She doesn't leave.
"But I just bought the jar.
It was full."
"Yeah."
"So, those were special Greek olives.
They were expensive.
Imported."
"She said they were really good."
"Well, this won't do.
Not at all.
This will not do."
"Mom." I click off the TV.
"Mabel is worth
a jar of olives."

She stares at me,
then walks away.

"She's great, Dad."
We scootch Grandpa into bed.
"That is such a relief, Clare.
Mabel seems like a very nice person.
How's that, Lawrence?"
Grandpa nods.
Dad arranges his pillow.
I put the harmonica on his nightstand
with his glasses.
"Night, Grandpa."
"Sleep well," says Dad.
He flicks off the light,
and I follow him to the kitchen.
Mom's off-key voice
sings out from the shower.
Dad and I grin.
"Never did sound good,
but she loves to sing
and gives it all she's got." He laughs.
"Mabel used to sing professionally," I say.
"Really?"
"Yeah."
We load the dinner dishes into the dishwasher.
"That must have taken a lot of work."
"She didn't say. But I guess so."

I clink one plate against another.
"Here." Dad makes a space for me
to slip a dish into the rack.
"She said she didn't enjoy singing professionally,
so she sings for herself now."
"I can understand that."
I dry my hands on the towel.
"I never really thought of doing that before.
I thought that'd
kind of be like failing
or something."
Dad leans back against the counter
and looks at me.
"How can it be a failure
if she enjoys what she's doing?"
"Yeah. I know. That's what I'm saying."
"Good." He ruffles my hair.
"Dad," I moan.
He does it again.

In my dream
I'm dancing.
Not learning to dance
or working at the barre.
I'm really dancing.
But not on a stage.
It's Grandpa's garden.
I twirl faster

and leap higher.
I'm turned inside out
and feel as beautiful
as the flowers.
I can see myself.
Dancing.
Happy.

Could I?
In the morning
I plié at the end of my bed.
Shorts and a T-shirt sure let you move.
I frappé, grand battement,
and hold an attitude.
Could I, for myself?
I toe step over to the dresser
and tilt the mirror to see my face.
Could I?
I brush back my hair
and pin it into a bun.
Maybe
I could.

"Mabel, you don't need to do this," says Mom.
"Nonsense." She serves up breakfast
for Mom and me.
"Mr. Dwight and Mr. Lawrence

already ate. You two dig into those toads."
"Toads?" I ask, staring at my egg
in the center of a piece of bread.
"Toad-in-a-hole. You all never had this before?"
Mom and I shake our heads.
"The egg is the toad
sitting snug in the bread. Go on.
You can trust a girl from Mississippi."
We take a bite.
"Mmmm," we say together.
"Best toad I ever had," says Mom.
"Well, I don't know about that." Mabel
sets the iron skillet in the sink. "I've had
some good
frogs legs before."
"Eewwww," I say.
And we laugh.

Grandpa looks up from his morning TV show
to give Mom a kiss.
"Have a good day," she says to him,
"and be sweet to Mabel."
He smiles.
"What's that, Mom?" I ask.
"What?"
"That fancy notebook."
"Oh, that." She blushes
and shoves it farther down into her book bag.

"It's a blank book for writing.
If inspiration strikes or something.
If someone should happen to think of words
to write down.
It's for that."
I go with her to the front door.
Dad honks from the car.
"Writing what words?"
"Maybe some poetry.
A little haiku.
Cinquain.
You never know."
"Really? I never knew you wrote stuff."
She kisses me on the cheek.
"I don't,
but it's always been
sort of a dream."
"Cool."
I watch her hurry to the car.
Knowing Mom,
it won't be a haiku,
it'll be
an epic ballad.

"Let's load," says Mabel
from my bedroom doorway.
I look up from my magazine.
"What?"

"I got your granddaddy ready
and packed a lunch.
Let's go for a hike."
"Hike?"
"Sure. It's a treasure of a day."
She zips off.
A hike with Grandpa?
I pull on some socks and dig out
my hiking boots.
Who knows?
But I can't wait to find out.

"This van is a beaut."
Mabel pulls through the intersection.
"You okay back there, Mr. Lawrence?"
"Grumpphher."
"Good," she says.
"Are you going to be comfortable
hiking in your dress, Mabel?"
"Surely, surely."
"How are we going to hike anyway?"
"Most parks have a few paved trails
for wheelchairs."
"Really?"
"Uh huh. Sit back and enjoy the ride."
"Okay."
I have a feeling
there's not much arguing you can do

with Mabel.

My boots clomp on the asphalt.
We pass a few couples
on the trail.
"Afternoon," says Mabel.
The people smile
and head down the hill
as we head up.
Little alpine trees
line the way.
Massive meadows
roll down
to where Grandpa's van is parked.
It looks like a little green dot from here.

"Mmm. Smell that air,
Mr. Lawrence."
Grandpa and I
take a deep breath.
"It smells so clean
and light," I say.
"Yep."

Mabel rolls Grandpa up the incline
like it's no problem at all.
We take the final bend
and come to a broad, paved circle

with picnic tables.
The Olympic Mountain Range
surrounds us.
"Wow. Snowy peaks as far as you can see."
"Awesome and mighty," says Mabel.
We stand there and look.
It's like everything
is looking back
at tiny us.

"These sweet pickles are delicious."
I take another crisp bite.
"You a pickle lover?" asks Mabel.
"Definitely."
She pulls Grandpa closer to the table
and gives him another spoonful of yogurt.
"Will Grandpa always have to eat soft stuff?"
"Oh, I imagine he'll recover
some more of his swallowing ability."
"I hope so."

We unwrap a couple thick sandwiches.
"Thanks for bringing all this."
"You're welcome."

Two marmot heads pop up
in the grass.
One whistles, and they disappear.

"It's nice no other people are here," I say.
"Oh, I don't think so." Mabel wipes
Grandpa's lips.
"I think it's fun to meet new folks,
don't you?"
I shrug.
A gray mountain jay swoops down
and tears some crust off my sandwich.
His slender claws graze my hand,
then he's off.
"Hey!"
He flaps to a tree top.
Mabel and Grandpa laugh.
"I guess we aren't so alone
after all," she says.
"Nope."
The gray jay
blinks
and nibbles my crust.

Grandpa pulls out the harmonica.
"Play us a doozy, Mr. Lawrence."
Mabel gets to her feet.
Grandpa's notes slip and slide
into the air.
"Sweet," says Mabel.
She looks up at the pale blue sky
and sways.

Grandpa tumbles the notes out faster.
Mabel lifts her hands
high over her head and hums.
The skin shimmies
on the back of her arms.
The music seems to slide right
through her body.
Her pudgy feet take tiny steps in rhythm.
She's incredibly graceful.
"Come on, Clare," she says.
"What?" I grip the picnic bench.
"Come dance."
She sidesteps over,
takes my hand,
and pulls me up.
I'm stiff in front of this
large dancing woman.
What are the steps?
There's no choreography or anything.
Nobody to tell me what to do,
what step to take.
"I can't," I whisper.
"What do you mean you can't?"
This is stupid.
"Close your eyes," she says.
I do, but cross my arms.
"Listen, Clare. Listen to your granddaddy
singing to you."
"I can't."

"Be quiet and listen."
I do.

The notes press their way
through my muscles and into my bones.
I open my eyes
and see I'm swaying
to the same beat as Mabel.
I follow her little tiny steps
into Grandpa's song.
Over and over
with our arms lifted high.
I turn inside out
in front of
the huge mountains,
the marmots and Mabel,
the gray jay and Grandpa.

Grandpa breaks into the song
I danced to last year at my old school.
The Chinese one from *The Nutcracker*.
The beat flies at me fast.
I'm laughing out loud
as the steps storm back through my body.
Faster and faster
Grandpa plays.
Changement,
changement,

changement.
My boots thunk the pavement.
Double pirouette.
Triple.
And pose!
I collapse onto the ground.
Grandpa bangs his armrest.
"Bravo!" hoots Mabel.
"I'm-totally-out-of-breath," I gasp.
"You lost me back at that
first twirly-mabob," laughs Mabel.
"Wooo!" I lean against Grandpa's chair,
and he pats my shoulder.
I just
danced ballet.

The hills whir past
as Mabel drives us home.
Seems like I floated down the trail
back to the van.
Grandpa played music
the whole way.
Now his snores rumble.
"We tuckered out your granddaddy," says Mabel.
"Sounds like it."
She changes lanes.
"You sure seem happy, Clare."
I flip open the vent.

"You were dancing the likes I've never seen."
"Only an old ballet routine I performed
last year."
I tug my seatbelt looser.
"Did you like performing?" Mabel asks.
"It was okay."
She raises the rearview mirror a bit.
"Well, I could tell you love to dance.
Someone along the way
has believed in you.
You've obviously had wonderful training."
"Yeah. My dad and Grandpa.
And Mom.
They supported me for years.
I used to spend a lot of time learning.
But not anymore."
"Well, you weren't learning anything
back there. You were dancing.
I know. Same kind of passion comes over me
when I'm singing."
"Really?"
"Don't you know? Clare,
you need to have yourself
some space and time to dance now."
I grip the arm hold
as the van bounces in and out
of potholes.
Grandpa sleeps through it.
"I got kicked out of my old class

because I'm too tall."
"Well then, take a different one. Must be
something somewhere
for you to dance to. You sure wouldn't want
to lose all that joy
because someone else
thinks you're too tall."
"But I won't ever dance ballet professionally."
"Probably not." Mabel speeds up
and merges onto the freeway.
"But you'd be dancing
for yourself."

If I'm not good enough
to be a superstar in New York,
and I'm too tall for City Ballet,
is it right
or fair
to want to dance
anyway?
Do I deserve the chance?

I open my bedroom door
and peek out.
The stir-fry sizzles in the kitchen.
Mom laughs at Dad's joke.
I turn and shut the phone book.

The lady I talked to was nice at least.
My hand shakes
as I circle the dates and times
of the adult class on my notepad.
I could still take class
Monday through Saturday if I wanted.
The cost is so much less
than we paid before,
with lessons only an hour long.
Only flat shoes are used,
so there'd be no toe shoe expense.
I flop on my bed and pull my feet up.
And no blisters and bleeding.
There's probably a couple people in class
with a little talent.
For sure Grandpa wants me
to keep taking lessons.
What would Mom and Dad think?
What do I think?

I match my domino on Mom's train.
"Thank you." She adds a tile
to mine.
"Your turn, Dwight," she says.
"Yes, yes."
Grandpa is totally focused on the game.
"So I called Ballet Conservatory today."
"Oh, good." Mom looks at me. "Did we have

any outstanding bills?"
"I don't know. I didn't ask."
Dad places a domino.
Grandpa matches one onto his train.
"What did you call for, then, Clare?" says Dad.
"I, you know, was asking
about the adult class
in case I ever wanted to maybe
take one sometime."
The three of them
look at me.

"Well, Clare," starts Mom,
"I thought we—you—had set that dream aside.
That you were going to look for a new pursuit."
"Yeah. But maybe for some exercise
or something. What do you think, Dad?"
"Excellent idea."
"But, Dwight. We all know
that class is unprofessional.
Remember that one time?
We saw them
when we were waiting for Clare's class to begin."
"I remember."
"Well then, you know what I mean.
The form and technique are shoddy.
What's the point, Dwight?"
"The point, Martha,
is that Clare loves to dance.

And it looked to me
like that class was there for the same reason."
Grandpa grunts his approval.
"But there's no goal or end."
"Mom." I lean forward. "There doesn't
have to be."
She rearranges her dominoes.
"Is that possible? I mean, after the failure—"
"It wasn't a failure, Mom!"
I bang the table and the dominoes jump.
"Clare!" she says.
"I was good enough for the company."
She takes a deep breath. "But you're
too tall, honey."
"Yeah. So I am. Too tall for their
cookie-cutter corps.
But I'm not too tall to dance, Mom.
It's what I want to do."
"Glad to hear it." Dad folds his hands. "Now,
do you have a play, Clare?"
I check my tiles.
I set down a double five on Mom's train,
click my last on the table,
and play it on the double.
"I win."
I get up and walk away
from the stupid look
on Mom's face.

I rock on the porch swing.
Clouds skid away from the moon.
Mom never went for her dream
till now.
Maybe she didn't
really have it before.
I wonder if she's only writing
because she thinks one day
she'll write a book?
A collection of poetry?
And then everyone will want to buy it.
And she'll win some award.

What if she never sells a word?
Does that mean it's a waste of time?
Why can't doing the thing
be the goal?
Where the fun is.
Everyone should get
to do the thing.
Like Grandpa still skiing
when he was too old and slow
to win any more races.
He kept doing it
as long as he could
because he loved doing it.
I'm not good enough for New York,
but this is who I am
and what I want to do.

That's the way it's going to be for me
from now on.
As long as I can.
The best I can.
Dad and Grandpa understand
my dream now
is to dance.

While I'm waiting for the popcorn
to finish,
Dad comes in.
"I want some water," he says,
and fills his glass.
"Thanks, Dad, for being so cool
about the adult class."
He takes a long drink
and wipes his mouth on a napkin.
"I always said failure is not your future."
"If I work hard enough, I'll learn something
along the way."
"Exactly." He sets his cup in the sink.
"Far as I can see, you've learned
you are a dancer
who loves to dance."
I make myself look him in the eye.
He comes over and gives me a hug.
"And don't worry.
I'll talk to your mother.

When is the next class?"
"Tomorrow."
"You going?"
"I want to."
"Then I'll stop in on the way to work
and settle the costs."
Beeeeee, squeals the microwave.
Tomorrow!

I kissed Grandpa good night,
and Dad gave me a hug
before I went to bed.
Mom called out
"Good night" to me.
I called the same back.
We were really
still yelling at each other.

I hear crying in the night.
Who is it?
I rush to Grandpa's room.
He's sitting up in the dark,
weeping.
I flick on the light.
"Grandpa, what is it?"
He points to his right arm and leg.
I sit down on the edge of his bed.

He reaches over,
grips my hand,
and presses it to the dead side of his face.
His tears are warm
from both eyes.
"Grandpa, I'm so sorry."
He gasps in air.
I tug out a tissue and dry his face
and mine.
He lets out a big sigh
and looks over at
his old hymn book on the nightstand.
I pick it up and flip to the bookmark.
"The one by Medley?"
He grunts and lies down.
I read aloud,

>"Whene'er my Saviour and my God
>Has on me laid his gentle rod,
>I know, in all that has befel,
>My Jesus has done all things well."

I look at Grandpa.
His eyes are closed,
and he's smiling.
I lean over and kiss him
on the forehead.
"Clare, is everything all right?"
Mom clutches her robe
in the doorway.
"Yeah."

I go over to her.
"Grandpa's okay."
I flip off the light.
"He's okay."

He's changed.
Different
and the same.
I'm changed.
Different
and the same.
We can sit and remember
how good it was,
hiking,
skiing,
getting ready to audition,
and be
sad.
Or
we can be
who we are now
and
try to enjoy the new parts.
We are both trying.
I know that
for sure.
Grandpa said
he could always count on me

to try.
I must have
gotten that
from him.

The adult class is before my old class.
I'm up early with excitement,
even before Mabel gets here.
I tug my dance bag
down from the top of the closet.
My knee bumps the tube of posters,
and it clatters to the floor.
I toss my bag onto my bed.
Maybe I'll hang the posters later—
at least Baryshnikov.
I grab clean tights and a leotard
from the dresser.
They slip on easily.
Today I don't feel like a sausage at all.
It's more like my ballet clothes
are hugging me just right.

I start brushing out my hair.
"Clare?"
Mom opens the door and steps in.
"Can I help you with that?"

I shrug. "I guess."
She draws the bristles
over my scalp.
"I didn't sleep well last night."
"Sorry." My sarcasm sneaks out.
"Your dad and I talked
late into the night.
I wanted to really try and see
what you two were thinking.
But it's completely different
from the way I've always thought."
She hits a snarl and gently works the brush
to untangle it.
"Clare, being the best and winning
were extremely important to me growing up.
Dad won so many ski races,
and he and Mom were always top performers
in the Puget Sound area
for ballroom dance.
They were so good at everything.
I allowed myself to be too scared to try
anything at all.
I was afraid of them
seeing me fail."
She looks at me in the mirror.
"I'm sorry I said you failed, Clare.
Not making City Ballet
had nothing to do with your effort."

"Thanks, Mom."
She winds my ponytail
into a bun
and slides in the pins.
"I'm proud of you, sweetheart."
She tucks a stray hair behind my ear.
"I'm proud of you for knowing
who you are
and doing what you want."
I turn and hug my mom.

She brushes a tear off her cheek.
I pull my toe shoes out of the bag.
The blood stains on the boxing
are brown.
There's already a musty smell.
"I guess I can leave these here."
I go to set them on my dresser.
"Wait." Mom takes them from me.
"Why don't you display these
in Grandpa's cabinet?"
"I don't know, Mom."
"Clare, you wore these. This is probably
your last pair of toe shoes.
I'm proud of what these represent."
"What's that?"
"A dream you reached for.
Hard work.

Perseverance.
Sacrifice.
And most of all,
love
for ballet."
"Okay, Mom.
Let's find a spot for them."

Mom moves some ski ribbons
and dusts the shelf.
I unwind one shoe
and slip it on.
The narrow flat boxing presses into my toes.
I teeter on the hard leather sole.
It never did seem wide enough
to support my whole foot.
I go up on pointe.
Crunching
pain.
I roll down
and slip off the shoe.
Who ever invented toe shoes
anyway?
Dancing on pointe is totally unnatural,
unhealthy,
and painful.
"Hand them to me," says Mom.
I quickly wind the ribbons

and put both shoes in her hand.
She places them
on the shelf
right under the light.
The glass door clicks closed.
"Perfect." She gives me a squeeze.
"Dwight, we need to grab some breakfast," she calls,
and hurries off.
The pink satin shines through the glass.
But there's dust,
blood, and sweat
on them too.
This is the perfect place.
I don't need them
to dance
anymore.

"You know," says Mabel,
feeding Grandpa a spoon of oatmeal,
"since I don't work Sundays,
I bet Clare could take Mr. Lawrence
to church." She winks at me.
I filled her in yesterday.
"I'm sure I can," I jump in.
"It's right down the street."
Even Grandpa grunts a yes.
Mom and Dad look up from their cereal
and say, "Okay," before they even

think about it.
Nobody argues with Mabel.
Besides, it's too important to Grandpa.
After last night, that's for sure.
His religion comforts him.
And I'd kind of like to know
what that's about.
Sunday
I'm
taking him.

Mom and Dad were giddy
going off to work.
They hung out the car windows waving
like this was my first dance class in my life.
"Good-bye, my little ballerina," called Mom.
"Have fun!" yelled Dad.
I hugged myself and enjoyed every second of it.

Mija perches on the porch
and cackles at the goldfinch
swooping by.
"You go, chickpea!" Mabel sings out
from the swing.
Grandpa waves super hard,
making his wheelchair rock.
I step through the gate.

This feels bizarro.
Things are still changing so fast.

I pick a blueberry from the hedge
at the end of the street.
The sweet tang
is perfect.
I hurry to the conservatory.

I wait for the light.
Isn't that Rosella in the coffee shop
with her mom?
Definitely.
They look right at me.
Rosella's mouth is hanging open.
They probably can figure I'm going
to the adult class.
I wave. Might as well try.
Her mom pulls her away from the window
immediately.
Oh, come on.
The light changes.
I keep my head up
and cross the street.
So her mother
doesn't want us to be friends.
No doubt there.
Maybe I can say hi

between classes,
when her mom isn't around.
If I don't act embarrassed,
then maybe she won't
feel embarrassed.
I hope Rosella's okay.
She needs a friend
really bad.

I spring up the steps.
The handle is smooth.
I grasp it
and pull.
The door opens,
and I step in.
Music swirls out of the classrooms.
My heart skips a beat,
but today
it's because I can't wait
to dance.

"And one and two." Madame
claps the beat for a class of little girls.
I hug the wall and aim for the dressing room.
Before I step through the door,
I look back.
Madame holds my gaze

and mouths, "Welcome back, Clare."
I smile,
shiver,
and go to change.

"Well, hey there," says the fuzzy red-headed lady.
"Hi."
"Are you joining our class?"
I nod.
"Well, great. My name's Janet,
and this is Susan, Claudia,
Jayni, Christie, Dani, and Cathy."
All the women say, "Hello."
"Hi."
I pull off my jeans and slip on
my shoes.
It's absolutely weirdo
to talk to everyone.
But it's also kind of nice.
My hand brushes the bottom of my bag.
"Rats."
"What?" asks Janet.
"I, I guess I forgot my skirt."
"You know, I have an extra.
Here. Let me look." She digs through her bag
and pulls one out.
"Thanks." It's blazing yellow.
Yellow!

"Try it on."
"Okay." Why not?
"That looks great."
"Thanks."
I hurry out to the barre.
Their niceness is going to take some time
to get used to.

The barre room is empty.
I choose a sunny spot and stretch.
It feels warm and comfortable.
The yellow skirt makes me laugh.
"What's so funny?"
I jerk around.
"Elton!"
He leans on the barre. "It's great to see you."
"What are you doing here?"
"Same thing as you.
I take adult class sometimes
just to dance."
"Oh." I look everywhere but at him.
"So, what was funny?"
"This skirt. It seems crazy
because it's so yellow."
"It looks great."
I look up at him. "Thanks."

The rest of the class join us:

a bunch of men, women, and a few girls my age.
The teacher with the goatee comes in.
"Hi, Mr. Pike," calls one of the ladies.
"Hello to all," he answers.
"Let's begin with pliés, shall we?"
Elton whispers, "This teacher is the best.
He loves teaching this class,
and you are going to love him."
The lady pianist begins.
Same one as always in the barre room.
She must play for everybody.
In first position,
I port de bras with my arms
and flow into the rhythm.
I'm doing pliés,
and I'm dancing already.
I'm turned inside out
by a simple exercise
because
I'm dancing
for myself.
We finish the right side and turn for the left.
Elton brushes my hand.
"Beautiful," he says.
I know it.

Willow

I'm Mother's *prima ballerina*. Every single second of my life she reminds me. Ballet is our passion. But I'm really, really tired, and it's time for my next class. Already.

Rosella

I can't believe Clare is taking adult class! Mom kept saying that's so pathetic. But Clare looked happy. I wish we were still friends. But man! Right now I really wish whoever's in the bathroom would get out so I can purge before class. And I still need to get a couple bandages on my toes. The skin is barely hanging on. Hurry up already. I have to puke!

Dia

I'm fat. I can't stand to look at myself in the mirror because I know what I should look like, and I don't. I hate ballet, but I'll always want to look like a stupid ballerina.

Margot

Is there anything out there besides ballet? Something else I could do? It doesn't matter. It's time for class.

Elton

I'm so glad Clare is taking adult class. Everyone in here will dance better because of her. She's beautiful to watch. I'll be watching.

Clare

I am a dancer.

Made in the USA
Lexington, KY
17 February 2019